KAYLEE BALDWIN

ME & MR. JUST RIGHT

ENCHANTED FORRESTERS

KAYLEE BALDWIN

SWEETLY US PRESS

For Jo, who always gets me to dive in head-first and gave me an adventure of a lifetime.

1

LIA

*L*ia gripped her seat's flimsy armrests as the puddle jumper jerked through heavy turbulence. Cups of soda flew into the air, throw-up bags were flung down the aisles by buckled-up crew members, and passengers' panicked howls sounded worse than Friday night karaoke.

In another life—the naïve one Lia had lived until last month—she might have appreciated the symbolism right at her fingertips. Mined it for poetic images and lyrics her fans could mine even deeper for personal meaning.

She hummed in rhythm with the bumps of the plane, then added words.

Turb-ul-ent pl-ane ride.

Tur-bul-ent life-uh.

Someone screamed in a high F-sharp. Too high for Lia's range. Impressive.

Back to the song. What rhymed with turbulent? Gent, vent, rent ... Ugh. She tipped her head back and closed her eyes. *This is how my career ends—with bad lyrics and worse metaphors.*

What if her ability to write a meaningful song was yet

another thing Bo and Gwen—*oh, excuse me,* Bowen—took from her?

The plane jerked her into the window and then into the muscular arm of the man beside her, and she took the opportunity to breathe in his woodsy scent. (*Wait! Turbulent scent! Ugh. Stop.*) Men's cologne smelled better in Alaska.

The men were more ruggedly handsome in Alaska too. Take that, Nashville.

Lia'd been stealing glimpses of this man's tan arm from the corner of her eye since he'd sat beside her, fascinated by how his sun-kissed forearms flexed with every bump.

"Have you been to Alaska before?" Mr. Ruggedly Handsome asked, his friendly smile open and uncalculating. She narrowed her eyes. What was his angle? Other than brief hellos at the beginning of their flight to Winterhaven, they'd been happily ignoring each other for the last twenty minutes. Lia readjusted her mask, securing it more firmly around her mouth and nose. Without her huge sun hat and enormous sunglasses, she felt exposed, but no one had recognized her. Yet.

Not everyone knows who you are. The snooty voice in her head sounded like Gwen. Who didn't want their backstabbing ex-best friend as their critical inner voice?

"I went to Palmer a few years ago," Lia said, mostly because if the plane *did* crash, she didn't want Gwen's voice to be the last thing she heard.

"Did you see the reindeer farm?" His low tone was calming, even as the plane dropped several feet.

Her grip tightened. She never should have come here. She never should have trusted anyone, ever. She should have insisted the airline let her bring her guitar as a carry-on. It was her emotional-support guitar.

"It's just outside of Palmer," he continued. His warm, rosewood-brown eyes stared at her expectantly, and she breathed through her spiral. *Reindeer farm.*

"No. It was a quick trip to the fair." Early in her career, Lia'd opened for Jimmy Ricky at the Alaska State Fair. The memory brought mixed feelings. She'd spent most of the trip arguing with her overbearing mom-turned-manager, but it had also been the first big crowd she'd ever sung to. It had been incredible to have an audience sing along and scream for her. They might have bought tickets to see Jimmy Ricky, but in that moment, they'd been there for her too.

Would Lia do this all again, knowing what she knew now? Before, the answer had been an unthinking, resounding yes. Now? Her breathing hitched as she realized she couldn't say yes anymore. And it wasn't just that her boyfriend, Bo, and her best friend, Gwen, had a secret relationship behind her back for months. It was that they'd stolen an album's worth of songs Lia had co-written with Bo, and then rushed to release them.

Lia had expected to feel ecstatic to see her best friend's success. But not this way. Not with her songs. Not with her boyfriend. And not after Gwen shared so much of Lia's personal life with the press. Had any part of their friendship been real?

"Never thought of the Alaska State Fair as much of a destination." Mr. Ruggedly Handsome chuckled as if he hadn't a care in the world, a stark contrast to pretty much everyone else on the plane. Except his right hand betrayed him. Seeing his white-knuckled grip on his armrest put her at ease. Like, between the two of them holding on to their armrests, they could keep the plane from going down.

Also, it made her feel less dramatic. *You always overreact.* She shook Gwen's commentary away.

"At least you're fixing your perception of Alaska by coming to Winterhaven," he said in that magical, calming voice. He turned to look at her, and those brown eyes gave her something to focus on besides the plummeting plane. "It's one of the most gorgeous places on earth. You'll see when you get there—but everything is more vibrant, and the sun is paradise on your skin."

"What else?" she asked, then clenched her jaw against a scream as the plane dipped again.

He continued to describe the town of Winterhaven, with it's adorable shops and friendly community. Winterhaven might be amazing, but if Lia lived through this plane ride, she'd have to see it another time. She was taking a boat straight from Winterhaven to a tiny, unnamed island near Thorne Bay as soon as this plane landed.

A tiny, unnamed, *unpopulated* island where she could be off the grid, all by herself, alone. No tabloids. No paparazzi. No surprise radio plays of Gwen's new hit single. No images of Gwen and Bo locked in a passionate embrace with alliterative headlines like *Borelia's Bitter Breakup*. And no more seeing that ridiculous celeb mash-up of Lia and Bo's names. The fact that Bo had liked it was a red flag she'd missed. Among many, many others.

The vacation rental hostess had apologized for the lack of Wi-Fi and cell service on the island, except for one tiny spot on a hill—if the stars aligned and the clouds parted and the fish flew in rainbow formation, or something like that. The only reliable communication Lia could have with the world was with a satellite phone. She couldn't book it fast enough.

Just Lia and nature for one whole week.

But that wasn't the kind of information you divulged to a complete stranger, even if his rumbly voice made you want to curl into him like a kitten, *and* he smelled, inexplicably, like sunshine.

Especially not then. Lia took him in carefully. How did Mr. Ruggedly Handsome feel about celebrity mash-up names? That was her new litmus test for how much to trust someone from now on. If they liked them? Red flag city.

Oh, Lia. So optimistic, thinking you'll trust people again.

The plane lurched, a soda cup rolled past her feet, leaving a sticky brown line in its wake.

"If you get the chance, make sure you head to the beach at low tide."

She tore her gaze from the soda staining the corner of her canvas bag. "Why?" Her throat was dry.

"If I told you, that would ruin the surprise." He gave her a mischievous smile, and the stranglehold her fingers had on the armrest relaxed. Perhaps he worked for the Winterhaven Tourist Center. Or he was the mayor or something, because he clearly loved this town. "Also, if you have time, look for the bookstore—it's in a Victorian-style home—and stop by Alaska Chic, an art boutique a stone's throw away from the bookstore."

Focus on those dimples. "Any book recommendations?"

"What do you like to read?"

"Poetry. Historical."

He leaned even closer, like he was divulging a secret, but also like he was trying to block her view of the woman across the aisle crying hysterically. "They have an entire Alaska section. You really can't go wrong there. For fiction, I love *The Snow Child*. For nonfiction, they have several collections of journals from travelers, or guides for animal and plant life in southeast Alaska."

Lia didn't pull away, even though she should. Mostly because she didn't want to see the crying lady, but partly because this close, she could see the tiny freckles on his nose that added a unexpectedly boyish touch to his face. "Are you trying to distract me?" she whispered.

His lips twitched into a half smile that made her stomach squeeze. "A little bit. Is it working?"

"A little bit," she repeated. If the last sight she saw was those eyes, well, there were worse ways to go. "I fly often, but rarely on planes this small."

"I take this flight at least once a month." He relaxed back

into his seat, to her disappointment. He peeked over his shoulder at the crying woman, who was being comforted by her seatmate, before looking back at Lia. "It's pretty rough at least half the time, but we always make it okay. And the reward of Winterhaven is worth it. Don't let the clouds fool you. Southeast Alaska is paradise."

"You live here?"

"Sometimes."

What did that mean?

Before she could ask him, the pilot's voice came over the speaker. "Sorry about all that bumping around, folks. Welcome to Winterhaven, Alaska. Local time is 1407. Weather is sixty-five degrees and cloudy, but I see some sun poking through. We'll have you on the ground in about fifteen minutes."

The plane evened out enough for Lia to put her hands in her lap. Mr. Ruggedly Handsome gave her a crooked grin and turned to the crying woman across the aisle. He took her hand and started deep-breathing exercises that the older woman copied until her shuddering breaths calmed.

When the plane landed, more than one person cheered.

Lia's seatmate indicated that she should precede him from the plane while he waited for the panicked woman, who looked extra pale. Just before exiting, Lia couldn't resist peeking back to find him hauling bags down for an older couple. Men like him didn't exist in her world.

She stepped from the plane and descended the stairs to the tarmac, inhaling a deep breath of cool air. July in Alaska might be heaven. Though she loved Nashville—well, she did, *before*—she didn't hate escaping summer's wet cocoon of heat.

A light mist fell from the sky, and Lia slung her soda-dampened bag over her shoulder as she followed the passengers out to the front of the trailer-turned-terminal. She stayed apart from everyone, facing the road, until their bags were carted to the trailer.

Her soul sighed with relief when she spotted her guitar on top. This guitar predated Bo and even Gwen. Most of Lia's songs were written with her fingers strumming over that body. She snagged it from an airline employee and knelt to open the case to assure herself it was, in fact, in one piece. It had survived the Winterhaven Plane Incident in Lia's Heartbreak Tour. Or, what would her PR firm, her manager, her recording studio, and her family call this adventure if she'd told them about it? The Pity-Party Tour? The She's Lost Her Mind Tour?

The Sour Grapes Tour, Inner Gwen whispered.

Regardless, the invite list had one person on it: Lia Halifax.

She closed the case and then did what she should have done the second she'd stepped off the plane—rifled through her bag for her floppy hat and oversized sunglasses. Armor on, she scanned the parking lot and spotted a young woman standing in front of a dark blue truck, holding a sign that said "Lia."

She was much younger than Lia expected—early twenties, maybe. She wore cutoff shorts with a black hoodie, and her long auburn hair was pulled back into a high ponytail. Most of all, Lia adored her waterproof boots. She'd turned down the cuff to reveal red-and-white octopus fabric beneath the latex.

"Rose?" Lia asked as she approached.

Rose's eyebrows winged upward as she took in Lia's hat, sunglasses, and mask. "One and the same!" she said, her expression full of mirth. "Ready to hit the road?"

"Absolutely." More than ready. Lia climbed into the truck, and Rose peeled out of the parking lot as if the cops were on her heels. Lia tried to imagine what her manager, Carmen, would think of her getting into a car with a stranger in the middle of nowhere, thick woods followed by endless ocean on all sides.

She'd throw an absolute fit. Which was why Lia hadn't told her anything. Only her assistant knew where she'd gone this week—and she was perfectly capable of fielding all the phone calls and texts coming her way, while keeping Lia's location secret.

She was definitely going to deserve a raise.

"What brings you all the way out here?" Rose asked over roaring wind blowing through the open windows. Lia held her mask to her face so she didn't lose it. Rose glanced quickly at her, then back at the road. "You can take your mask off out here."

"I'd prefer not to," Lia said politely but firmly. Let Rose think she was rude. Lia craved anonymity like she craved carbs whenever her team put her on a diet. Meaning: desperately.

Rose lifted her brows, clearly taken aback.

Lia softened the edge to her tone. Rose was not her enemy. "I'm here to get away from everything." How much could she say without giving too much away? "My life recently imploded."

"How?" Rose asked, her shoulders relaxing. "If you don't mind me asking. My brothers are always quick to tell me that I'm a snoop." She rolled her eyes. "As if their lives are interesting enough to snoop into."

Lia laughed. She hadn't talked to her brother since Christmas. Lucas was only nine years old, and she could only have so many conversations with him about Lego creations and video games.

"My boyfriend cheated on me," Lia said. That was universal enough of an experience to be safe divulging it without sparking any recognition.

"No!" Rose said, perfectly indignant.

"With my best friend," she continued, comforted by Rose's reaction. So many articles had hinted *Lia* was to blame. Like being famous meant you deserved to be betrayed.

Rose gasped. "Stop it."

"And then spread a rumor ... at work, that I'm unstable. After they stole my work and took credit for it."

Rose pumped the brakes so hard, the seat belt tightened over Lia's chest as she flew toward the dash. "I'm going to need names and addresses. My brothers might not be good for much, but together, we can get this job done."

Lia coughed and settled back into her seat. She peered over her shoulder to make sure no cars were behind them, but the road was empty. And she was apparently alone with an aspiring hit-woman. "Ummm ..."

Rose laughed. "Sorry. That's Mr. Hyde talking."

"Mr. Hyde?" Lia asked.

"From the book? *Strange Case of Dr. Jekyll and Mr. Hyde*. He's the murderous alter ego. *I'm* only murderous in theory. I promise." She held her fingers up in two peace signs and gave Lia a cheesy grin.

Lia relaxed. She liked Rose, who reminded her a bit of her younger sister, jumping from topic to topic like a frog on a lily pad. It was easy for Lia to sit back and listen. Plus, Rose gave off good vibes. *So did I*, Gwen whispered.

Rose pressed on the gas and they were on their way. "My brother, Jules, says my dark humor is why I've never been in a steady relationship."

"Well, relationships aren't all they're cracked up to be."

"Right? Thank you! *None* of my brothers are in steady relationships, but Jules doesn't give them any grief. It's a total double standard."

"Stay single as long as you can," Lia advised. Maybe that would be the theme of her next album—with her hit single, the brilliant song "Turbulent."

You'll never write again, Inner Gwen whispered.

Rose parked her truck at a marina and led Lia down a sloped metal walkway to the docks. The scent of salt and fish met Lia as they approached a yacht with a red-and-white dinghy parked beside it. "Here's our ride. This is your last chance to check your phone, because you won't have reliable service out there."

Lia had turned her phone off when she'd gotten on the plane in Ketchikan, and she had no intention of turning it back on again until this week was over.

Rose took Lia's bag and guitar and placed them on the seat, then helped Lia onto the little boat. The engine started with a hum, and Lia turned to rest her arms on the back of her seat to watch Winterhaven retreat.

Maybe by the time the week was over, everyone in the world would've forgotten that Borelia had ever existed.

And maybe Lia could figure out where to go from here.

2

HAYDN

aydn heard his sister's truck peel out of the airport parking lot before he saw the white decal reading Alaska Chic—the name of her boutique in downtown Winterhaven—across the back window.

Close call.

He loved his baby sister, but Rosie was a bit like a frozen lake. Beautiful and serene—until the ice cracked and the water sucked everything down into its frozen depths. He'd already blocked off a week to help Rosie in her store, *after* he spent the next week with his brothers, but until then, it was better if she didn't know he was in town.

She could be intense, and this week needed to be about relaxing, connecting, and helping Bennett get out of his funk. And most of all, it was about convincing himself he'd done the right thing by turning down the offer to be an exclusive features photographer for *Nature Adventure Magazine*.

Sure, they'd offered him twice what he was earning as a freelance photographer for *Alaska Ridges Magazine*. And a chance to explore all of the United States, all expenses paid. And his own online journal via *Nature's* website, with a monthly print byline. But he'd have to relocate to Los Angeles. Which was a nonstarter. He might leave his family for a month or two at a time to photograph different parts of Alaska, but he'd never up and leave them permanently. Not like their father had.

He grabbed his bags—the last on the cart. He'd learned to keep his camera and computer with him at all times, but his tripod was checked on, along with his clothes.

"Thank you again." The older woman who had been screaming was one of the last remaining people at the airport, along with her adult daughter. "I don't know what got into me."

"Everyone was panicked, not just you," Haydn assured her.

"Well, you were very helpful," her daughter said. "Is there any way we can repay you?" Her gaze flickered down to his bare ring finger, and her smile widened.

"No repayment needed," he told her gruffly. Haydn had a strict no-relationship policy for himself. His lifetime commitment load was overflowing with his siblings alone. Taking care of them was a full-time job. And, most importantly, he wouldn't ever put himself in a position to have to leave someone he loved, which—with his wanderlust genetics—was always a possibility. "Have a wonderful time in Winterhaven." His phone buzzed, and he glanced at the screen. "Oh, this is an important text. I've got to grab it."

The woman and her disappointed daughter waved, exclaiming at the sight of a bald eagle, while he strode away and read his brothers' text thread:

> **BENNETT**
> You've got mail.
>
> I hear nothing. Not even a sound on the streets Winterhaven.
>
> **JULES**
> Just the beat of your own heart?

BENNETT

Yessss!

Haydn groaned. It was going to be an entire week of this. Whole conversations in cheesy movie quotes, led by Bennett. And he loved it—not that he'd ever admit it.

HAYDN

Who even sends emails anymore?

JULES

We do at work.

HAYDN

I meant romantic emails.

JULES

Excuse me? Interpretive law emails are the epitome of romance.

HAYDN

Talk lawyer to me.

BENNETT

People email all the time. I get like 100 a day.

HAYDN

Exactly. So it's not special. My heart has never raced over an email.

JULES

I turned off my email notifications.

HAYDN

Me too.

BENNETT

You might miss the love of your life emailing you.

HAYDN

It's a risk I'm willing to take.

JULES

If she doesn't text, she's not the love of my
life.

BENNETT

On my way, H.

I'll email you when I pull up.

Haydn laughed and toggled over to his news app to pass the time until Bennett got there. It was only a few minutes' drive, so there wouldn't be much time to kill.

The top news story was—yet again—the scandal and dramatic breakup of superstar country singers Aurelia Halifax and Bo Benton. "Un-Hinged Halifax!" the headline read, and the article was subtitled: *Exclusive report: Former best friend, country singer Gwen Winstead, details the mental instability of Aurelia Halifax and gives insight to her breakout album, 'Love Awakened.'* Beneath the headline was a picture of the blonde Aurelia Halifax, mascara and eyeliner streaked around her sad, bloodshot eyes and her lipstick slashed messily across her full, scowling lips.

He couldn't imagine being on stage in front of so many people—both literally and in the news like this. Haydn scrolled past the story to read the national news headlines before giving in to the urge to open up the *Nature Adventure Magazine* app. Why was he torturing himself like this? He'd turned the job down. They'd already offered the position to a friend of his, the one he'd suggested they reach out to. Still, he scrolled past photos of the Grand Canyon and Niagara Falls. Imagined the views and readership he'd have with *Nature*.

The toot of a tiny horn saved him from himself. Bennett rolled into the parking lot in his ridiculously small truck— which was paid off, as Bennett always reminded him—waving through the open window. His unkempt beard had taken over the entire lower half of his face. That was new.

"Get in, loser."

Haydn rolled his eyes as he grabbed his duffel and camera bag and slid into the passenger seat. Bennett, always the hugger of the family, threw his arm around Haydn's shoulders. *This* was what being home felt like.

Bennett navigated the truck onto the two-lane street. "How was the flight?"

"Rough. Tears were shed."

"Yikes. Anyone faint?"

"A woman across the aisle from me was close. And my seat-mate was shaking." He'd lost sight of her while helping the older woman. The mask hid her mouth and cheeks, but her eyes had been kind and intelligent.

He'd always been a sucker for that exact combination.

Despite the mask, she was the kind of gorgeous that couldn't be hidden. In fact, she'd looked familiar, though he couldn't place it. It wasn't like he ran into a lot of women in the remote reaches of the Alaska wilderness. And since she'd never been to Alaska, other than the state fair—he shook his head at the travesty of it—they couldn't have met before.

"Jules flies into town tomorrow morning, and then we can head out."

Haydn frowned. "I thought he was coming tonight."

"Something came up last minute." Bennett shrugged. "We're lucky he didn't cancel completely."

"Hmm." That was a loaded hmm, and they both knew it.

Bennett drove the long way around town, circumventing the downtown shops where Rosie—and his ex—worked, to get them to his tiny, one-bedroom house. They hiked up the rickety platform stairs, and Bennett scrunched his nose as if bracing himself before he opened the door.

It looked even worse than Haydn had prepared himself for. Clothes strewn across the furniture. Old to-go food containers on the counter. Dishes spilling out from the sink. Dust on the closed blinds.

"It's been rough," Bennett said, taking in the scene as if through Haydn's eyes. "And don't give me any of your 'romantic relationships aren't worth it' garbage."

"I wasn't going to say that," Haydn said, even if he was thinking it. He knew when to keep his thoughts to himself. Haydn squeezed Bennett's shoulder affectionately. "Good thing I'm here before Jules."

"Yeah, he'd probably condemn the place. Rosie already tried to burn it down."

Haydn snorted. "She didn't."

A reluctant smile creased the corners of Bennett's mouth. "She was trying to light a candle to help with the smell, and one thing led to another." He toed aside some clothes to show where a hole had been burned into the carpet. "She swears it was an accident."

"Right." They exchanged a knowing look. "I'm here now." Haydn was the most levelheaded of the siblings. His ability to be calm in the face of any disaster was one of the qualities that made him a good nature photographer. And a disaster this was. "Why don't you run to the grocery store and get all our food for the week? I'll get started on this."

"I don't know." Bennett shook his head, even as he palmed his keys and edged out the door. "You sure?"

"If it's up to me to get the food, we're eating hot dogs and trail mix all week."

Bennett shuddered. "How are we related? Don't feel like you have to do anything around here. If you need to rest or catch up on work—"

"Oh, believe me, you can't make me do anything I don't want to do."

They all knew that was true. As the oldest brother, Haydn

was generally used to giving the instructions and not the other way around.

Bennett loped down the stairs without a backward glance as Haydn surveyed the mess. See? His brothers needed him. He couldn't move to the lower forty-eight and abandon them. Right now, his houseboat was docked in Ketchikan, near the larger airport, but he could easily bring it to Winterhaven for a few weeks or months. Get his family settled again.

He slipped his black hoodie off and threw it over the stair railing, then grabbed a trash bag from under the sink and started to clean.

3

LIA

*L*ia caught her breath as the house on the island came into sight. It was even more gorgeous than the pictures online had shown.

It was made entirely of redwood planks, with a light gray trim at the peak of the steeply pitched roof. A railed porch circled the house, with a recessed porch area on either side of the front door. She squinted and could see a white swing bench beneath the overhang. It was close enough to the ocean that the house would have amazing views, while being just set in enough that she wouldn't have to worry about waves.

Best of all, though, were the floor-to-ceiling windows surrounding the house. She pictured herself sitting by them, taking in the gorgeous scenery while strumming her guitar. She hugged the case to her, relieved she'd brought it. She'd walked out of her house without it initially, but then made her driver pause last minute so she could run inside and grab it.

She couldn't let them ruin music for her.

Lia and Bo had met when he'd opened for her on her last tour. They'd immediately clicked—he'd been so charming—

and it hadn't taken long for them to start collaborating. Their duet single hit the top of the charts, as did their next one. It only made sense when their relationship slipped seamlessly from professional to personal, and the unwieldy beast, Borelia, was born. Their fans went wild, and their relationship increased both of their fame exponentially.

She could see now that Bo was using her. Gwen too. She'd started out as one of Lia's back-up singers four years ago, and they'd become fast friends after touring together. Gwen was the one who'd encouraged Lia to invite Bo to open for her. How long had they been seeing one another behind her back? Had they planned on stealing her songs all along?

And which idea was worse: that they'd planned this from the beginning and none of it was real, or that they'd really loved her once but chose to betray her anyway?

Lia had written music long before Bo and Gwen came into her life, and she'd continue now they were out of it.

If only they were *really* out of it. That would be much better than the lies they were spreading about her. She'd never trashed a hotel room or refused to pay her dancers. And though she sometimes wrote songs about past relationships, she'd never once stalked a past boyfriend or sabotaged a new relationship he was in.

Yet people loved drama, and they could twist her words to mean something she didn't intend. Bo had to know it was a bad look for him to be caught cheating on Lia. Plenty of people didn't like her music, but there was a reason she'd been photographed for the cover of *Fame Sensation Magazine* last spring with the headline "America's Darling."

Now she saw headlines claiming she was "Unsteady in Life" —a play on her most downloaded song, "Unsteady in Love."

Stop, Lia. She'd come out here to forget her worries for one week, to be off the grid in a way her life never allowed for. She eventually needed to go back home, talk to her label about pushing back her album's release date, rewrite an album's worth of songs, and reclaim the narrative somehow.

So, you know, just some small, no-big-deal things.

Before she tackled any of that, she needed this week in the same vital way she'd always needed music. She breathed chords and melodies the same way everyone else breathed oxygen.

"This is one of my favorite places on earth!" Rose yelled over the sound of the engine. She held her nose up in the air. "And that scent of pine trees along with it? Divine."

"It's gorgeous!" Lia couldn't wait to pull her mask and sunglasses off and let the sun hit her face fully.

They pulled up alongside a homemade dock Rose tied the dinghy to. Lia took Rose's outstretched hand for balance as she climbed onto the dock. "Let me give you a quick tour." Rose motioned across the waterway, where Lia could see a few other houses in the distance. "These are your closest neighbors. Most of the residents only come here seasonally. That one is owned by a man who likes to vacation out here when he can get off work, and he may or may not be there this week, but I wouldn't plan on it."

The houses were weather-beaten but stunning in their own right. One was bright green, another bright blue.

She recalled what Mr. Ruggedly Handsome said on the plane, about everything being more vibrant here. She understood now what he meant. The magic of the mountains and the clear Alaskan air transformed even the mundane into something spectacular.

"This is the Forest Chateau." She turned back to the house Lia would be staying in for the week. She pulled a phone from a clip on her waist. "Before I forget, here's the SAT phone. It's mostly for emergency use. That said, don't hesitate to use it if you need to."

"Okay." Lia shivered. From excitement? Nerves? Maybe she was adjusting to the cold, coming from a Tennessee summer to an Alaskan one. She'd never been so disconnected from the world. She'd always been the kind of person who needed people. Yet trustworthy people were in short supply these days.

"I have the numbers for the closest neighbors in a kitchen drawer, so you can call them if you need anything. Also, my number is on there as well. Let's see ... here are the check-out instructions." Rose rifled through her pack and pulled them out. "I'll pick you up Sunday." She gazed out at the horizon and bit her lip. "It looks like a storm is heading this way. Are you sure you don't want me to leave the dinghy?"

"How would you get home?"

"Good point." Rose blew air out from between her teeth.

"I don't know how to drive it anyway," Lia assured her with a shrug. "And I have no plans of going anywhere." She wanted to sleep the entire week away, if possible.

Rose grabbed the grocery sacks she'd stashed in the back of the dinghy, while Lia got her belongings, and the two headed into the house to get settled. Rose chatted easily about her life while she unloaded groceries for Lia: her boutique, her new employee who spent more time on her phone than working, the cute son of the bookstore owner, and her annoying brothers, but she said it so affectionately that Lia could feel her love for them. Lia appreciated the steady stream of friendly noise as she settled into her new house for the week.

What would it be like to be so open with someone? Anything Lia said could be used against her, and she had learned quickly that she needed to keep her secrets guarded and her thoughts secure, or else she'd be reading some hyperbolic version of them in the tabloid headlines the next day.

Too quickly, Rose said goodbye, and Lia listened to the sound of the dinghy crossing the water. And then she was alone.

She slipped off her damp shoes and stuck them in the closet by the door, and then she wandered through the house to take it all in. It had a coconut-musk smell. Kind of manly, but clean. The kitchen was huge, with a vaulted ceiling and wide open spaces for the gray marble counters. This was designed by someone who liked to cook.

Lia didn't cook well, hadn't needed to cook for herself in years, so she'd sent Rose a list of foods that were easy-prep meals—salads and fruits and even her favorite sugary cereal she rarely ate anymore.

She warmed up a cup of soup and ate it with one of the deli salads from the market. She sat at the back window as she ate, and watched the waves flow past the house.

After eating, she played her guitar for hours, until the tips of her fingers were numb. Every time she stopped, the quiet of the house felt like too much, and she'd start to play again.

It stayed light outside until almost eleven, and she still felt a buzz of energy. Without thought, she reached for her phone to distract her. The blank screen reminded her that even if she wanted to turn her phone back on, she didn't have service. Perhaps coming here had been a mistake. She hadn't realized how all this quiet would give her too much brain-space to think. And the last thing she wanted to do was think.

She'd lost her best friend and her boyfriend. She'd let her guard down; she'd let them in. It made everything so much more painful when they'd left.

She took one of the sleeping pills her doctor had prescribed for when she was on the road and her schedule was all over the place, and then sat in front of the bookcase in the living room. It was filled with Alaskan stories—from adventures to historicals to romances and everything in between. Her gaze caught on *The Snow Child*, the book Mr. Ruggedly Handsome had told her about. Her fingers skimmed over the blue spine, and she tugged it from the shelf. She hadn't read a novel in years.

She dove right into the atmospheric story, reading until her eyelids drooped and the words swayed on the page. She'd placed her belongings in the biggest bedroom, with the king-sized bed. She wandered down the hall to it. Her entire body ached with exhaustion. Sleep had never sounded so divine.

She threw herself across the bed, expecting heaven, but was instead met with something akin to a hospital transfer board. "Oof," she groaned, grabbing the back of her head. This was the worst bed she'd ever lain on. She rolled around in an attempt to find a comfortable position, but the only way she felt halfway decent was on her back, and she hated sleeping on her back.

Had they bought the cheapest beds they could find? The big, plush couch in the front room was really comfortable. Perhaps she'd sleep there.

She poked her head into the second room to check, and was pleased to find a queen-sized bed with nearly a dozen pillows and a down comforter.

She didn't jump this time—she'd learned her lesson already—but slowly lowered herself onto the edge ... and kept lowering even lower.

That was nice. Really nice.

She sank into one of the pillows, closed her eyes, and stretched out every limb. She tried to roll onto her side, but it was impossible. She was in quicksand, and it was slowly absorbing her into oblivion.

She flung one leg over the other and heaved her body to the side of the mattress, feeling like she'd gotten a workout in just one move.

Yeah, that was not going to work either.

She dropped her arm to the side and squeezed the mattress. There had to be at least three inches of foam atop it. Who in the world could sleep like this?

She struggled to sit up and finally pitched herself onto the floor in one unglamorous heap. She stared at the slanted bedroom ceiling. Perhaps this cabin was like a carnival's fun house—deceptively beautiful but designed to disorient and confuse you. Rose did seem like the kind of person who would get a huge kick out of bringing in beds made to torture poor, unsuspecting tourists.

She sighed. Should she even check the last bedroom?

Curiosity and anticipation—when had her life come to the point that mattresses excited her?—had her jumping to her feet and going to the final room. Perhaps this one would be a waterbed. Or a bed of nails. Maybe even a cradle.

To her initial disappointment, she discovered a twin-sized bed topped with a navy quilt and two sensible-looking pillows. She pressed her hand down on the mattress to test it out. She knew better than to trust any bed in this house.

So far, so good.

She sat and bounced a few times. It had a good amount of cushion, but not so much that she felt like she was going to need to say goodbye to her loved ones before she fell asleep. Nor was it so hard that she would need to cancel her next tour while she recovered from the muscle aches.

She lay back and the mattress nestled her perfectly. Every muscle relaxed as she rolled from side to side to make sure she could.

This bed? It was just right. She'd slept on some expensive beds over the years, and this rivaled those. It was just her size, with the exact right amount of padding, pillow, and blanket. Like it was designed for her. It even smelled divine—somehow exactly like sunshine.

"Sorry I doubted you, Rose." Her eyelids fluttered with exhaustion. What a day. She was here. In Alaska. Not quite knowing what she was looking for—it had to be more than disconnection from the world—but hoping she'd find it anyway.

Hoping. The word caught in her mind. Perhaps that's what she came here for. Hope.

She climbed under the quilt and soft sheets, and before she could continue to contemplate her past, her future, or any space in between, she was fast asleep.

4

HAYDN

*H*aydn hoped the sea-salt spray sure to fly in his face during the boat ride to the cabin would have the power to wake him fully.

Bennett had arrived home from the store right about the same time Haydn had set the last filled trash bag on the curb. He'd vacuumed, washed the dishes, and taken three loads of laundry—including Bennett's sheets—to the laundromat a few doors down.

Bennett had come bearing dinner as well, and the two brothers had stayed up long into the night talking. Bennett had an old air mattress he pumped up for Haydn, which collapsed around him approximately two hours into sleeping on it. Haydn wasn't that old, but he was definitely too-old-to-sleep-on-the-floor old.

They'd picked Jules up from the airport just before eight in the morning and headed straight to the marina. Rosie's yacht was parked in her usual spot, making Bennett's tiny fishing trawler seem like a hummingbird beside a hawk. The waves were already at three feet, and based on the incoming clouds, they were only going to get bigger as time went on. Haydn loved a good, strong storm—once they were at the cabin. He didn't want to hit anything too big while they were out on the water, which meant it was past time to head out.

"It's going to be a bumpy ride, boys," Jules said. He hopped into the trawler with the grocery bags hooked around his arms. Of all of the brothers, Jules was the most athletic. He'd played basketball all through high school and college, before injuring his knee bad enough that he decided to retire his sports dreams and go into law. He'd kept up his workout regimen, though, and it showed.

Haydn was no slouch in the muscle department. His came from hiking and climbing and exploring the wilderness, but still, he had nothing on Jules.

Bennett's muscles came from lifting people off their feet when he gave them bear hugs. And also from reeling in huge fish day after day. But mostly the hugs.

"Let's get there quickly." Haydn loved the fishing trawler. There was nothing like being *right* on the water, feeling every single wave below your feet.

They set off with a whoop. It was an hour-long boat ride to their cabin, which gave them all enough time to decompress from work and phones. Even Jules, who sent one last email in the car, had turned off his phone and was keeping an eye out for sea animals.

Every time they came through here, they saw something: seals, whales, otters, sea lions ... and it never grew old. One might think, growing up in Alaska, a person would become accustomed to seeing the wildlife, but not the Forrester brothers. Or Rosie. She created stunning pieces of art for her boutique, based on the animals around the bays.

It was difficult to talk over the noise of the boat, but they didn't need to be talking for Haydn to finally feel settled. This, here, was his happy place. The wide, open sea. Fresh air. And best of all, being with Jules and Bennett.

He loved traveling. He loved it too much. It was good for him to remember that he loved *this* more. Their dad's restlessness had turned him into a resentful man who'd finally left. And if Haydn sometimes felt restless too, well ... being restless wouldn't define him. It wouldn't compel him to leave. He sometimes struggled with that balance of living his life to the fullest without betraying his family, but he was succeeding. Mostly.

Guilt tugged at him for avoiding Rosie in Winterhaven and not inviting her along. He promised himself he'd spend the entire next week with her, one on one, which was better for her anyway, since she and Jules didn't always get along.

He needed his brothers this week to help him out of this funk he'd been in since he'd turned down his dream position—not that they knew about the job offer or how he'd passed on it.

Bennett needed them to help him through his broken heart—without Haydn's commentary on how his no-romance policy had never left him crying over burnt carpet and empty food containers. Even if it was true.

And Jules? Just like he played basketball on a bad knee until he nearly destroyed it, he'd work without break until he keeled over at his desk unless Haydn and Bennett stepped in. They'd already lost both parents. No need to lose a brother too.

Haydn pulled three granola bars out from his hoodie pocket and passed them around. Having grown up on these waters, none of them got seasick, even in massive waves, something they all happily exploited by eating heartily on the boat.

By the time the house came into view, Haydn was fully awake and excited for the week ahead. Multiple houses dotted the little islands in this area, and summer brought the part-time residents and vacationers.

Jules jumped out of the boat to tie it to the dock, while Bennett slowly navigated the boat as close as he could get to the boards.

Haydn inhaled the scent of island crispness. Nothing

smelled better than the air at their cabin. The brothers had all built it themselves over the last ten years. They'd started it after their dad left. This island, this house, was a part of them.

They grabbed the groceries and bags and did the short walk up to the cabin. Jules unlocked it and went inside.

"Who was here last?" he called over his shoulder to Bennett and Haydn.

"Me. Why?" Haydn had overnighted there three weeks earlier, when he'd first gotten the job offer for the new magazine. He'd thought a weekend at the cabin would help him figure out what to do, remind him why he couldn't accept.

Haydn and Bennett went straight to the kitchen to set down their food. In the kitchen sink were a bowl and a plate, rinsed off, but not all the way clean. Haydn winced. He was usually a clean person, but he had been distracted that week. With them not being in the house very often, he had to be careful about putting food away so no mice or other forest animals would make claim to their house.

"Dude, you left food in the fridge too." Jules grabbed Haydn by the neck and rubbed his knuckle playfully into his head, while Bennett took the opportunity to take light potshots at his stomach.

Haydn was an adult. A professional. A respected photographer. But he would always be their brother. If he didn't love it, he'd definitely have to hate it. He twisted out of Jules's hold and grabbed both of them around the neck to wrestle them down to the floor.

Unfortunately for him, he was the smallest, and they made quick work of slamming him to the ground. He groaned but smiled. Rosie would be calling them puppies right about now, before she threw a full cup of water on them and went running for the forest. She was small but competitive, and with three older brothers, she'd learned to play dirty.

"What's first?" Haydn asked from his spot on the ground, feeling winded. "Fishing or hiking?"

As if nature had heard his hope, the skies opened with a crack and rain poured down.

"Made it here just in time." Jules went back to the kitchen to finish putting away the food. "We've still got to get our bags from the boat."

They glanced out the window and the darkened skies, and then all three scrambled outside to get the rest of their things. They were all soaked in short order.

"I wouldn't mind a rainy hike," Bennett said as he dropped his sopping wet bag on the floor. He loved being outside more than any of them, regardless of weather.

"I'm up for it, but I want to put different shoes on," Haydn said.

Jules hesitated.

"Don't be boring," Bennett warned him.

"Is it boring to not want to be wet and cold?"

"Yes," Bennett and Haydn said at the same time.

Jules merely shook his head and snagged his bag to head to his bedroom. "Hey!" he called down the hall. "Maybe next time you sleep in my bed, you could make it before you leave."

"I didn't sleep in your bed." Haydn huffed as he went to Jules's doorway. "You have terrible taste in mattresses. I'd rather sleep on the floor."

Jules snorted.

"You must have forgotten last time we were here," Haydn insisted.

"Unlikely," Jules said. He'd been working on a huge case last time they were here together, but even a stressed-out Jules wasn't a forgetful Jules.

"Haydn. The gig is up." Bennett stuck his head out into the hallway from his room. "You seriously went through and messed up all our beds? That's not even a clever joke."

Haydn shook his head. "I would have put a fake snake in your bed, but what would be the point of just messing it up?"

"Exactly." Bennett huffed. "Man. You even got dirt on my sheets? I'm going to have to wash these before bed." He pointed his finger at Haydn, his expression annoyed. "We like pranks, but not lazy ones. Do better next time."

"But I didn't—"

Bennett shut his door in Haydn's face.

Nothing like being with his brothers to make him feel like a teenager again.

Haydn opened the door to his own room last, threw his bag on the floor, and went to sit on his bed to take off his shoes when something made him pause.

Or, more accurately, *someone*.

Because there in his bed, sleeping deeply, was a beautiful woman.

5

LIA

*L*ia awoke to the sound of quiet male voices. She rolled over and blinked, disoriented. Where was she?

"Should we wake her up?" a man said.

She sat up quickly and pressed her back to the wall, awake enough to remember where she was. A deserted island. All by herself. In the middle of nowhere. Without Wi-Fi or cell service —except for that magical hill she hadn't taken the time to find. Alone.

Except apparently not.

She still felt groggy from the sleeping meds and staying up until almost two in the morning. She was used to staying up late, but being out here, it was like she'd lost all sense of time. Rain pounded on the window, and the gray light was still bright enough for her to know that it was morning. Or afternoon.

Why didn't she have her watch on? Oh, right. Because she'd thrown it in the trash in Nashville when it wouldn't stop sending her notifications about Bo and Gwen.

"Let her sleep."

"But who is she?"

As slowly and quietly as she could, Lia slid her legs off the bed and onto the floor. Her socked feet didn't make any noise as she stood. If she escaped the house, where would she go? She didn't have a boat. She imagined these men did, but she wouldn't know how to drive it.

She'd left the SAT phone on the couch last night. If she could just get to that, she could call ... someone. Rose or emergency services.

"Do you recognize her?"

"She looks familiar."

Lia peered around the door to see three gorgeous men in a huddle right outside the bedroom. The tallest one snagged her attention first. He wore a scowl on his angular face, the kind of face made for magazine covers under a headline like "America's Top Twenty Boardroom Hotties." His dark, almost black hair was nearly shoulder-length, and she knew expensive jeans well enough to spot that he had on a very pricey pair.

The second man was a little shorter and softer, but still strikingly handsome. His hair was a lighter shade of brown, and he'd pulled it back into a ponytail that looked windswept. Half of his face was covered in facial hair that appeared to have veered wildly past two-day stubble and into *I lost my razor* territory.

The last one, the one with the sandy-brown, shoulder-length hair, had his back to her. He wore a form-hugging hunter-green T-shirt, dark gray basketball shorts, and worn-out slides. The other two men were barefoot, which was a weird detail to notice but made them appear a little less threatening somehow.

They might be there to kidnap her, but at least they were considerate about not getting mud on the floor ...? She shook her head at her own ridiculousness. Well, they could go barefoot all the way to jail.

She crept toward the door. She needed a plan. If only she

could go back in time and keep the SAT phone with her. Or her shoes.

Or, as long as she was fantasizing about time travel, not come to Alaska at all. Not believe Gwen when she said she was just extra busy. Not give in to Bo's intense flirting and slick charms.

Never go to Nashville in the first place.

She loved playing guitar, she loved singing, and she loved writing songs and engaging with an amped-up crowd. But everything else that came with it—the fame, the paparazzi, the broken hearts, the people assuming you didn't have feelings because you were famous, all of that—she wished she didn't have to experience anymore.

She'd have to run. Run out to whatever boat these three had come in, and hope for the best. She was in great shape from all of the dancing she did on tour, but these men looked like they were in great shape too. Hopefully they were slow.

"The only way we'll get any answers is to ask her," the one with his back to her said. All three men squared their shoulders and turned toward the door.

She paused, stunned as their eyes met. She knew the hunter-green shirt guy. He was her seatmate from the airplane. Mr. Ruggedly Handsome. *Had he followed her?* This was worse than paparazzi. This was a stalker situation.

With a large inhale, she grabbed her water bottle and unscrewed the top, and as the men took a step toward her, she surprised them by flinging the water on them, throwing the bottle, then darting past them in the fastest, most adrenaline-filled run of her life.

"Hey!" one of them yelled.

Beside the front table, a pair of keys sat in a bowl. She hoped it was boat keys as she grabbed the set and yanked the front door open. She'd only made it one step onto the wooden slats of the front patio when a strong, tanned arm wrapped around her middle and jerked her to a stop.

Mr. Ruggedly Handsome, she mentally growled.

She fought with everything she had, kicking and screaming, and if she could turn around, she'd have bitten him. "Let me go, you stalker!"

"Stop! Calm down!" He held her firmly, but his grip didn't hurt, even as she knew her kicking had to be leaving bruises on his shins.

"Women don't like to be told to calm down," Beard-man said. "It makes them want to punch us in the face."

"Right. But she can't take off with your trawler."

"Not in this storm," the stern-looking one said.

They argued back and forth about if she could, in fact, take the boat she didn't know how to drive, into a storm that was already making her shiver.

She yanked herself from his grip. "Why are you following me?"

His brow furrowed, much like it had when he'd comforted the old woman on the plane. "I didn't follow you. I don't even know who you are."

"Ha!" she scoffed. Her mind worked through the possibilities. "On the plane, you must have figured out who I was and —" Her heart raced, her socked feet were soaking wet from the rain, and her body was shaking with adrenaline and cold. To her horror, her eyes stung with tears. "I'm going to have you all arrested for this. Stalking. Kidnapping. Assault. Ruining my vacation. Whatever they can get you on."

Recognition flickered in Mr. Ruggedly Handsome's eyes. "You sat beside me on the plane."

"And then you followed me here." She paced backward a step, relieved when none of the men pounced on her again. "I'm leaving. Don't come after me."

"That weather is turning fast," Mr. Ruggedly Handsome

said, in that same tone of voice he'd used to calm her down on the airplane. "Even with a lot of boating experience, I think it's a bad idea to go out right now." She followed his gaze to see a large boat rocking on the choppy waters.

She clutched the boat keys like a lifeline and walked out into the rain. Her foot came down on something sharp, and she cried out. Mr. Ruggedly Handsome tossed his slides over toward her. Not too proud to reject them, she slid her socked feet into the too-large sandals and marched toward the boat. She got to the dock and watched as the wooden platform rolled around on the waves. She didn't even want to step on the dock, much less get into the boat.

And why should she have to?

She swiveled around to see the three men still standing on the porch, watching her under the overhang that covered them from the worst of the rainwater drenching her to the bone.

They were the ones who'd woken her up from a good sleep, who'd come into her quiet space that *she* had paid for and were ruining her quiet alone time. They should go away. Not her.

Besides, she was *not* leaving her guitar.

She stomped back to the house, and their conversation abruptly stopped when she got within hearing range. "You three need to leave. I'm staying."

Mr. Ruggedly Handsome pushed his long, damp hair away from his face, showcasing his muscular triceps, as he exchanged an entire silent conversation with the other two men. "How did you get out here?" he asked her. Thankfully, he hadn't seemed to notice her perusal of his arms. "There's no other boat at the dock."

"Someone dropped me off." She folded her arms. Why was she answering their questions? They needed to leave, and she desperately needed to get inside where it was warm and dry.

"But this is *our* island. We own the entire thing," the bearded one said in surprise.

"I rented *this* house for the week," Lia insisted, but she blinked. They owned the whole island? That couldn't be right. "Maybe the rental company messed up the dates, but this is what I paid for."

Mr. Ruggedly Handsome shook his head. "We don't rent our house out."

"I can show you the invoice on my phone ... which isn't working because there's no Wi-Fi," she finished, her voice fading. Lia's mind spun, and she reached out to hold on to the railing as she suddenly felt dizzy.

Nothing could be easy. Not even her remote island getaway.

Oh, poor little famous rich girl crying about life not being easy, Inner Gwen mocked.

"It all adds up," Mr. Ruggedly Handsome said, his jaw tight and so different than the easy smile he'd had on the plane.

"What does?" Beard asked.

He ticked off his fingers. "Vacation rental. On our island. Us coming unexpectedly without telling anyone. And other times we've come to find food occasionally gone. Beds not made. Items sometimes broken ..."

The three men looked at one another with varying levels of annoyance on their faces, and in unison, they said a familiar name that finally put her at ease. "Rosie."

6

HAYDN

The woman looked like she was one wrong word away from bolting again—and Haydn still hadn't decided if he'd actually let her take the boat out in water like this.

No. He couldn't let her. Which maybe did make him a kidnapper. Or at least a withholder? Holding someone against their will, but for their own good? He winced. That would go over real well in court, for sure.

"Rose Forrester?" she asked.

They all looked at each other and nodded. Yep. Confirmed it was their sister who'd gotten them into this mess. "Let's go inside and figure this out," Haydn suggested.

Jules stalked inside first, followed by Bennett—who headed straight to the kitchen, probably to stress-cook. Haydn walked in behind them, his ears perked for the sound of the woman following them into the house at last. Relief dropped from his shoulders like a weight vest after a workout.

While Jules went to get the SAT phone from his room, Haydn grabbed a blanket from off the back of the couch and tossed it to the shivering woman. She wrapped it around herself without hesitation, though she still didn't leave the doorway. Wrapped in a huge blanket, her dripping wet hair tucked inside of it, and wearing his sandals—which were several sizes too big for her—she appeared extra vulnerable.

She noticed him studying her, and her chin lifted in defiance. He recognized her now, from the plane, and she was even more stunning without the mask, though her stay-back vibes were palpable.

"You know Rose Forrester?" she repeated.

"She's our sister. I'm Haydn," he said, hoping introductions would put her at ease. "Bennett's in the kitchen, and Jules is getting the SAT phone."

"Welcome," Bennett said as he filled a kettle with water.

The woman tucked the blanket even tighter around her shoulders. He backed away to turn on the gas fireplace. He generally didn't turn it on in the summer, but they generally didn't have a freezing cold woman here either.

"I'm ... Lia," she said, once his back was turned as he fiddled with the fireplace. She sounded a bit closer when she spoke next. "You really didn't follow me here?"

Why in the world would she think he'd followed her? She must know some pretty intense people to believe that could happen. Sure, she was beautiful. Gorgeous, one might even say —if they had room in their life to notice such things. But it still seemed extreme to believe he'd follow her all the way to this island. And creepy. Was he unknowingly giving out creeper vibes? He wanted to make it clear to women that he wasn't in the market for a relationship, not actually scare them. "I promise we didn't."

He grabbed a framed photo of the Forrester siblings from the entryway table to show her. Haydn had taken it right after the cabin was completed.

She took it from his outstretched hand and studied it. "I don't understand."

"Welcome to life with Rosie." Bennett placed four mugs on

the counter beside various brands of powdered hot chocolate. Bennett's solution to most problems was chocolate. The sweeter, the better. "Why don't you take a seat by the fire, and I'll bring you a drink." Bennett was the resident nurturer in the Forrester dynamic—his nurture method of choice being comfort in all forms.

She sat on one of the leather recliners but didn't relax into it. Her back remained straight, with her hands on her knees, the boat's key ring looped around her middle finger and clenched in her grip.

"This isn't our fault, Rosie," Jules growled into the SAT phone as he walked into the room.

They heard her tinny voice reply indignantly. "You didn't tell me you were coming to the cabin this weekend. You should have!"

"It. Shouldn't. Matter." Jules pulled the phone down to talk to the rest of them. "Apparently she's been renting out our cabin to vacationers when we're not here."

"It's not like you're using it," Rosie retorted. "It's going to waste, sitting there. And I clean it up when they leave."

"How long have you been doing this?" Jules asked, his tone steely, befitting a lawyer.

"Over a year," she said. "And making good money too."

"On our house!" Jules ran his hand through his hair in frustration, making the ends stick straight up.

Bennett and Haydn exchanged a knowing glance. Rosie had a way of pushing Jules's patience to the brink of explosion. Maybe it was because they were opposite in so many ways. Where Jules was a planner and executer, Rosie liked to be spontaneous and was the queen of starting projects she never finished.

As much as Haydn disliked that she'd been renting out their house without permission, he was reluctantly impressed that she'd been doing it for so long without any of them noticing.

"Let me talk to Rosie." Haydn waved his fingers for the phone. The way Rosie's breathing was hitched, he knew she was crying.

Jules tossed it to him.

"Hey," Haydn said to his sister, "we'll get this figured out, okay?" He walked a few steps away and turned his back to everyone, hoping they wouldn't hear Rosie's response.

He could almost see her shoulders slump when she spoke. "The extra income is what helped me keep the store afloat this year."

"You told me your new art was selling well." He checked in with her nearly every week, and he had offered more than once to loan her money to keep the store afloat, but she'd insisted she had it handled. *Don't hover,* she'd admonished him more than once. And so he hadn't, but this was what happened when he got too distracted. He'd been out of town too often, spending too much time docked in Ketchikan.

"Well, it was fine for a few months. And then it wasn't—and before you say anything, Haydn, I wanted to do this on my own."

"I could have helped."

"Right. Haydn's the glue. Bennett's the honey. Jules is the rock. And I'm the sour lemon," she said, sounding bitter. It was something their dad had said once, right before he left, like the world's worst parting gift, and it stuck like gum on the bottom of a shoe. Haydn didn't remember his dad actually using the word sour, but Rosie insisted he had.

"You're not a lemon. But for the record, lemons are amazing."

"The best of the fruits!" Bennett yelled out. They'd all had this conversation with Rosie multiple times.

"Bright and cheery," Jules growled, clearly still bugged, but he'd hated that statement more than any of them.

Lia's brows furrowed in confusion, but she added, "Lemon tea is my favorite."

Rosie huffed. "Well, whatever. But you know what really gets me? You three planning a trip together without inviting me. You left me out, Haydn. How lemony do you think that makes me feel?"

His guilt went from a small kitten's meow to a lion's roaring in his head. "I'm sorry. We shouldn't have done that. We'll make it up to you, okay?"

"Yes you will. By watching *Sleepless in Seattle* and *While You Were Sleeping* with me. All three of you. No complaints or mocking."

He cringed. Two movies with sleep in the title. Lovely. "Fine."

"At the cabin," she finished. "And I'm making a charcuterie board."

He tipped his head back and groaned. "Now that's taking things too far."

He actually didn't mind the charcuterie board, but it had become a joke among them. The first time she'd brought it out for the brothers, they'd all thought it was an appetizer and hadn't realized the crackers and cheeses and jams were the actual meal. They'd been hungry, she'd accused them of being uncultured plebs, and they'd still had to watch *How to Lose a Guy in Ten Days*.

"I guess I can forgive you," Rosie said.

Wait, how had he ended up being the one apologizing? Rosie had a way of twisting them all up.

"Don't do this again," he said, trying to sound stern, but mostly failing. "It's not fair to us, and it wasn't fair to Lia."

"Oh my gosh. Lia!" Her voice rose with worry. "She's going to leave me a terrible review."

Haydn pinched the bridge of his nose. "She's not going to have the chance to leave a review, because you're going to take the listing down."

She let out a huff. One beat of silence passed, and then another. Their best defense against Rosie, who hated silence above all things, was giving her the silent treatme—

"Fine," she said shortly. "I never meant for you to find out."

"Clearly." He chuckled, and in a moment she joined him, and then she groaned.

"Talk about worst timing ever. How is Lia? Is she okay? She was super skittish on the boat. Thought maybe she was running from the law or something, but her clothes were too designer for that."

He could hardly follow Rosie's train of thought on the best of days, much less when Lia's presence urged some inner part of him to tighten his stomach and flex his bicep as if holding the phone took a lot of muscle. "People in designer clothes run from the law too."

"It was her whole essence, Haydn," she said, like he was dumb for needing this explained. "Trust me. She's running from something, but it's not the law."

Unease settled over him. He turned to see Lia watching him. She knew he was talking about her. "If that's true, then imagine how she felt waking up in a house with three strange men."

"Strange being the operative word."

"Low-hanging fruit, Rosie."

"Sorry. I couldn't resist. But you're right. That would be horrible. Let me talk to her. I'd better vouch for you all. You might be a bunch of strange boys, but you're my *harmless* strange boys."

Lia bit her lip as he held out the phone to her, drawing his attention to her mouth. Her lips were pink and full—and he should *so* not be looking at them. She'd been studying him closely, but he wasn't sure what conclusion she'd come to about him yet. Lia took the phone into his bedroom to talk to Rosie privately.

Bennett brought him a mug of dark hot chocolate with raspberry. He'd made a caramel one for himself. Jules liked the mint-chocolate one. They drank plenty of coffee when they were out working, but here in the cabin, it was all about the hot chocolate. They'd taste-tested all the brands, all preferred something different, and had settled on the idea of being hot-chocolate hoarders. They had an entire cupboard dedicated to their stash.

"What do you think she wants to drink?" Bennett asked, staring down the hall.

How would Haydn know? But both of the brothers looked to him for an answer. "Uhhh, mint hot chocolate." A crowd favorite.

Bennett mixed it up for her and set it on the coffee table.

She walked back into the room, the phone dangling from her hand, and relaxed into the recliner. "Rose assures me that none of you are the torture-and-kill sort, so I guess I'll take her word for it."

Bennett nudged the hot chocolate toward her, and she took a tiny sip of it, wrinkling her nose in distaste. "You don't like mint, do you?" Bennett shot Haydn a glare as he stood, as if it was his fault he hadn't known a stranger's flavor preferences, and held out his hand for Lia's mug.

"It's fine," she assured him, but he just waved his fingers until she gave it to him.

"Not to Bennett," Haydn said quietly.

His brother was definitely in stress-cook mode. He dumped her drink in the sink, then rattled off all their flavors.

"Raspberry sounds wonderful," she said. "I honestly can't remember the last time I had hot chocolate."

"It's a cabin staple," Bennett told her.

"So what are our options for this house situation?" she asked as she took a steaming mug from Bennett and sipped it. A small sigh escaped—whether it was for the warmth or the taste, he didn't know.

What he did know was that he'd never been so mesmerized watching a mug press to someone's lips. He blinked his gaze away. *What's wrong with you, Forrester?* It was like he'd never seen a pretty woman before.

"I'll take you to Winterhaven as soon as the weather calms down, and you can catch a flight home," Jules declared.

A fire lit behind her bright blue eyes. "I can't go back yet."

"Well, you can't stay," Jules said.

Bennett, who had taken the seat beside Haydn on the couch, drank his hot chocolate down like it was fresh from the fridge and not steaming hot. Flecks of whipped cream caught in his beard. "She did pay for the week, fair and square. Maybe we should leave."

"Where would we stay?" Jules demanded. Actual vacation houses were booked this time of year.

"At my apartment?" There wasn't room for all three of them there. "Or on Rosie's boat." He grimaced as he said it. Rosie's boat was an amalgamation of projects that, like an artist's version of the Midas curse, seemed to multiply every time they were touched.

"This isn't a vacation rental," Jules said through gritted teeth.

"Lia clearly needs a break," Bennett replied. "Look at her."

They all did, and her cheeks turned pink. Her eyelids had the puffiness indicative of crying, and there were deep stress lines around her mouth. *Stop looking at her mouth, Haydn.*

"We'll pay the change ticket for you to go home early. And refund your money, plus ten percent for the inconvenience," Jules said, as if the decision were final.

"Money is not the problem," Lia said. "I need to get away

from … things." Her voice stumbled over that last word, and her gaze shot to the side as if she couldn't make eye contact. "And this is as *away* as I can get."

What could make a person so desperate to get away that she'd book a house on an island in the middle-of-nowhere Alaska? What—and why—was she hiding?

Rosie thought she was running from something, and the thought of sending her back to whatever it was she wanted to escape didn't sit right with him. But being trapped in a cabin with her … that didn't sit right either. Not with the way he kept *noticing* her. It was the stress of giving up this job getting to him. That's all. Still, it wouldn't be good to spend too much time with Lia.

A sudden increase in rain obscured the view of the beach outside the wall of windows, as if a bucket of water had been dumped on the cabin—and on their plans. They all three looked out the window as the sound of rain pattering against it increased.

Summer storms like this could last days. It was too dangerous to take the boat out right now, even if they could all come to an agreement about who was leaving and who was staying.

Even if staying here all together seemed like a very bad idea.

The lights flickered and went out. Gray sunlight filtered into the room, lighting it just enough to show the dismay on everyone's face.

"I hate to say this," Haydn said, barely biting back his own frustrated groan, "but no one's going anywhere today."

7

LIA

Tenseness settled over the room at Haydn's announcement. Lia hugged her hot chocolate closer to her chest, grateful for the warmth of both it and the blanket to act as a counterpoint to Jules's icy glare.

"Great," Jules grumbled. Lia couldn't agree more.

"It will be great," Bennett said, a little too cheerfully, as if knowing he needed to convince everyone. Whipped cream dotted his beard like snow on a pine tree. She patted at her lips to make sure she wasn't sporting a whipped cream mustache.

"It is what it is." Haydn said, slapping his hands on his thighs before standing up and heading to the fireplace, which still burned brightly. She was having a hard time getting a read on him, and every time their gazes met, he would quickly look away. It surprised her to realize she missed the easy camaraderie they'd had on the plane.

It was for the best that he kept his distance—that they all did. But that didn't mean she couldn't appreciate the way Haydn's shirt tightened across his shoulders and back as he fiddled with the fireplace knob. A knob she suspected didn't need to be messed with. She knew why she wanted to keep her distance from him—but it seemed he equally wanted to keep his distance from her. That was rare for her, and it definitely sparked her curiosity.

Maybe he's just not interested, Lia. Ever think of that? Inner Gwen said in a bored tone as she kicked her feet up on a desk and filed her nails.

"I know you from somewhere," Jules said, yanking Lia's gaze away from Haydn's delts. Jules didn't look or sound anything like Snape from the Harry Potter movies (maybe if Snape were young and muscled, perhaps), and yet... she couldn't help but think of him as Jules's gaze narrowed in on her.

"I just have one of those faces," she said in a falsely breezy tone.

What would happen if they recognized her? She got all kinds of reactions: people who felt the need to tell her they disliked her music, people who screamed or cried in shock, people who proposed on the spot, people who asked her invasive questions as if they had the right to know everything about her, people who became so starstruck they couldn't speak ... and on and on. The reactions were endless, but the result was always the same: she was never treated like a normal person again.

No matter which way these brothers reacted, it wouldn't be good.

"No, I know you from somewhere. Are you from Alaska?"

Haydn ran a hand across his mouth as he turned from the fireplace, toward his brother. "Jules," he said under his breath. It sounded like a warning.

"No," she said slowly.

"What's your last name?"

"Hall," she replied, staring back at him steadily. What was this? The Inquisition? The part in the movie where Harry gets detention?

From the corner of her eye, she saw Haydn tip his head

back to look at the ceiling, in the universal sign of someone grasping for more patience. "She's not on the stand, Jules."

On the stand. Was he a lawyer? She could see it. She'd worked with many lawyers over the years, with varying levels of hubris. Jules seemed like he would fit right in among the ones who thought the most highly of themselves—and who always underestimated her.

"I'm being hospitable. Getting to know our guest."

Guest. Riiiight.

"Where are you from?" he shot out quickly as if trying to catch her off guard.

"Tennessee."

"You look familiar to me too," Bennett said. And here she'd thought he was the nice one. "I can't place it, though. It's driving me crazy. Have you done a fishing tour in Winterhaven?"

"She's never been to southeast Alaska until now," Haydn said. He came back to the couch holding a camera he must have grabbed while she'd been in a staring battle of wills with Jules, and her heart stopped. She'd heard that phrase before, even written it in one of her songs, but had never experienced it until now.

She didn't know a lot about cameras, but she knew enough to recognize a very expensive, professional one when she saw it. Because she saw plenty of them, pointed at her.

"How do you know she hasn't been here before?" Jules asked Haydn, but his words sounded like they were coming from underwater.

The screen on the back of Haydn's camera lit up, and panic clawed up her chest. It wasn't that she couldn't deal with cameras—they were a part of her life. She didn't even mind getting her picture taken. But this felt like an ambush, on the level of finding out about Gwen and Bo's relationship. She'd thought she'd be safe out here, thought she'd finally have a moment of reprieve to process and grieve, thought she'd be granted one minuscule portion of privacy, thought—

"Because she told me." He looked up from his camera screen and smiled as if the two of them shared a secret.

Her heart started beating again, so hard it hurt. "When?"

His smile dimmed in confusion. "The plane. Remember? I pretty much saved your life."

"You were on the same flight?" Jules asked. "Way to keep that info to yourself."

"It's not like we've had a lot of time to talk," Haydn retorted.

"Why do you have a camera?" Lia asked. Or shouted, really. In an accusatory tone, as if asking him why he'd stolen all her new songs or betrayed her with Gwen or spread lies through the media about her.

Whoa. This time, her inner voice sounded like her and Gwen—and maybe her therapist—all rolled into one. *Not every man is Bo, Lia.*

Jules's eyebrows winged upward, and Haydn's brows joined his mouth in the downward-turn confusion party. "I'm a photographer."

"For *Alaska Ridges Magazine*," Bennett said, the pride evident in his tone. He leaned close to mock whisper, "He's kind of a big deal."

"*Alaska Ridges Magazine*?" she repeated, trying to soften her tone and slow her heart and somehow become a different person with significantly less baggage all at the same time. And while she was reaching for miracles—clear skies and an *actually* deserted island.

Haydn's cheeks were tinged with pink. "It's a magazine that features articles and photographs of Alaska. And I'm the opposite of a big deal. I'm the smallest of deals."

"He's won awards," Bennett continued as if Haydn hadn't said anything.

"Regional ones," Haydn clarified.

"And *Nature Adventure Magazine* even flew him out last month to interview him."

Lia's shoulders relaxed a smidge. Her stepdad loved *Nature Adventure Magazine*, and she knew it was filled with photographs of national forests and animals and interesting land formations, not celebrities.

"How did that go?" Jules asked, speaking for the first time in a while—and of course it was a question. The man could earn a gold in question asking.

"Oh, you know, boring subject, boring interview," Haydn said evasively, waving his hand and going back to flipping through his camera screen, so he missed the loaded look between Bennett and Jules. What was that about?

The silence stretched while they all waited for Haydn to elaborate, but instead, he stood and headed toward the kitchen, a restlessness to him that she recognized, having felt it herself so often. "I'm hungry. Anyone else?"

Jules looked like he was about to launch into another round of questions, so Lia spoke up quickly, surprising all of them, even herself. "I am. I haven't eaten today." Why was she stepping in to save him? He was a photographer *and* a vacation interloper—like, the two worst things combined. But as he'd said, he'd practically saved her life on the plane. Or at least her sanity.

He gave her a grateful look that his brothers had to have seen as well. The lights flickered back on, and even though it wasn't that much lighter, Lia exhaled with relief.

"I'm making lunch," Bennett insisted, bustling after Haydn. "Don't touch the shrimp, Haydn. I have it marinating for dinner."

Jules shook his head but then stood and followed his brothers, much to Lia's relief, leaving her alone. They bantered back and forth in the kitchen, and she discovered that Haydn had a reputation for not being able to cook more than hot dogs and s'mores over the fire.

She snagged her book from the night before and attempted to read, though she had a hard time focusing on the words. It was only a matter of time before one of them recognized her, right? But ... maybe not. These were three Alaskan men who lived alone, part time, on an island, who read nature magazines, not tabloids. If *anyone* wasn't going to know who she was, it might be them.

They set four places at the table with grilled cheese, tomato soup, and freshly heated cookies. Her stomach rumbled at the smell. She felt exposed leaving the huge blanket behind on the chair, like she was leaving her shield at the edge of the battlefield, but Lia really was hungry for the first time in weeks. Maybe it was the mountain air, or putting an entire country between her and Bo, but whatever the case, she realized, for the first time in weeks, she actually *wanted* to eat.

She sat at the table and was relieved to find they didn't require her for any conversation. It was relaxing, not being the center of attention and just getting to sit and listen without anyone caring what you might say next.

She made quick work of her sandwich, and Bennett slid the other half of his toward her. When she went to protest, Bennett patted his belly. "I think I'll survive without it, but I'm not so sure you will."

Her eyes watered, and she blinked it away rapidly. This was so silly. It was just a sandwich. Two triangles of sourdough bread with melted cheese. But no-strings-attached niceness was rare in her world. "Thanks," she said quietly.

"Week after next," Haydn said into the silence, "I'll be in Denali again if you guys want me to grab you some jalapeño cheddar popcorn."

Bennett threw his napkin down in mock disgust. "There he

goes, throwing it in our faces that he goes on adventures for a living."

"Photographers are insufferable," Jules said disdainfully.

"Going to the highest peak in North America again. Ope, and now it's glaciers," Bennett said in an awful, posh English accent. Had she ever heard the word "ope" in an English accent? She covered her growing smile.

"Oh, and fishermen are so much better?" Haydn asked, leaning his elbows on the table and bringing him just close enough for her to breathe in his cologne. When he'd sat beside her at the table, her stomach had swooped as wildly as the plane had earlier, but her hunger had quickly taken over any attraction she'd felt for him. Now that her food was gone, though, she had all the open thoughts in the world to consider Haydn. He threw his arms out as wide as they could go, and then lowered his voice. "Caught thirty fish today! At least twice this big!"

"They are at least that big," Bennett defended. "We're talking halibut here."

"But have you walked the glaciers like I have, multiple times?" Haydn asked with waggled brows.

Lia bit her bottom lip to keep from chuckling, but some movement on her part must have reminded Jules of her existence, because he turned to her abruptly.

"What do you do?" Jules asked her.

She didn't know what expression crossed her face, but Haydn reached across the table to grab Bennett's empty plate, blocking Jules's intense stare. "And all jobs," Haydn said, "are better than a lawyer who acts like house guests are on the stand."

"True dat." Bennett grabbed the other dishes, and they both ignored Jules's scowl.

"We used to call him the interrogator when we were growing up," Haydn confided in a quiet voice that was just loud enough for everyone to hear as he passed by Lia on his way to the sink. The nearness of him made goose bumps erupt on her arms.

Oh geesh.

Hopefully, no one noticed. Jules—who, of course, seemed to notice everything—watched Lia and Haydn carefully.

"At least let me wash the dishes," she said, "since you cooked for me."

The men didn't put up too much of an argument, though Haydn stayed beside her to dry the dishes after she washed them.

It was quiet without the chatter of the other brothers, who were both reading in their chairs in the living room. Jules read a huge brick of a book—historical, from the looks of it. And Bennett was nearing the end of a romantic comedy Lia would have loved to curl up with.

Lia and Haydn stood side by side at the sink, their feet bare. It felt surprisingly intimate—so domestic. So ... normal. He was about six inches taller than her, and his arm or hand would occasionally brush hers as she passed him another plate or bowl to dry. Did she sometimes slip her hand close so her soapy fingers accidentally brushed his dry ones? She'd never admit it, even under Jules's interrogation. Was she just craving kindness and touch—or was there something about Haydn specifically that felt grounding?

"I'm ruining you boys' week," Lia said, guilt pricking at her. If it was just as easy as finding a new deserted island to stay at, she'd leave, but she'd been lucky enough to find this one— which wasn't as deserted as she'd hoped. "It's a lot to get into, but if the rain lets up, I can't go home right now. Not yet."

"Do you want to talk about it?" He took a clean plate from her and ran a blue-checkered towel over it. "I'm a good listener."

She did want to talk about it, but then what? She didn't

actually know Haydn or his brothers. Didn't actually know if any of them could be trusted. More than anything, she wanted to forget any of it had ever happened. "I'd rather talk about you."

"I'm pretty boring."

"I have it on good authority that you're a big deal."

Haydn coughed out a laugh that made both of his brothers look up at him—Bennett with a curious smile and Jules with a suspicious brow furrow—before turning back to their books. "I have three fans—Jules, Bennett, and an old man who lives off the grid in the outskirts of Delta Junction. I bring him copies of my magazine and a homemade pie every time I come through town."

"You make pie?" she asked, surprised, because based on their earlier conversation, it seemed like he couldn't cook his way out of a bag of microwaved popcorn.

"No, but I am an expert pie buyer. One of the best, really."

"That is an undervalued skill in this world."

"Right?"

"What about Rosie? She's not one of your biggest fans?"

He shook his head. "Tragically, I'm the opposite of a big deal to her."

"Little sisters are the worst." She shook her head and laughed.

"Do you have a little sister?" he asked.

"Yeah, she's thirteen, and an expert eye roller. If I come up in conversation, she'll claim she's never heard of me." She clamped her lips shut. What was she thinking, letting that slip?

"Baby siblings, keeping us humble." He laughed. "Don't they know we have, like, three fans?"

"At least," she said. "There's a lady who owns a food truck by my house I always give a one-hundred-percent tip to, and she's a huge fan of me."

He whistled. "I waited tables in college. I'd be a fan of you too."

"I'll add you to my list." She pretended to write his name down. "But in all seriousness, I'm sorry this happened." She held her hands out to indicate the house.

"It's not your fault." He gave her a mischievous grin. "It's mostly Rosie's."

"You guys had no idea she's been using your house as a vacation rental?"

"Nope, but you'll notice that none of us are shocked. It's a very Rosie thing to do."

"You seem like good brothers." Even Jules, with his gruff exterior, clearly loved Rose. What would it be like to have a team of people on her side not motivated by money or fame? She'd lost two of the closest people to her in one fell swoop, and her family wasn't close like this. "Rose is lucky to have you."

Haydn's mouth slid into a determined line. "Exactly. And I'll always be here for her."

His words were weighted with meaning she didn't understand, but she nodded. "That's pretty special."

"I'm the glue," he said firmly. He peered over his shoulder to where the rain had let up just enough to see the wind whipping the trees around like wild horses trying to shake off their riders. "How would you like to explore an abandoned cabin?"

8

HAYDN

*H*aydn hadn't been able to convince anyone to go exploring with him until the lashing rain let up a bit. Now it drizzled like mist, perfect for an atmospheric hike to the old, dilapidated hunting cabin on the other side of the island. And double perfect as a way to avoid his brothers' questions about *Nature Adventure Magazine*. And *triple* perfect as a much-needed way to distract himself from how much he'd wanted to tug Lia into his arms when she'd looked up at him with a kind of longing that he knew had absolutely nothing to do with him.

She was clearly so alone, and so very lonely.

But his plate was full. He had nothing more to give anyone. He was tapped out on people to care about.

And yet ...

Haydn moved his belongings into Bennett's room and put on hiking pants. His legs had been cut apart by the spines of one too many devil's club leaves to want to mess with shorts.

He snagged his camera and his boots and headed out to the front to meet everyone. Bennett had already been dressed to hike, but now he also wore a lime-green waterproof bucket hat that he cinched under his chin. The logo for his tourist fishing company, "Forrester Expeditions," was stitched in red across the front.

"That's the ugliest hat yet." Haydn pulled on his hiking boots.

"Thank you." Bennett tugged on the ties dangling in front of his neck. "It's my bestseller."

"I can't imagine why," Jules drawled as he met them by the door.

"The uglier it is, the more my customers like it." He struck a vogue pose. "Don't hate the model; hate the fashion."

"There is no world in which this is the latest fashion." Haydn flicked the brim of Bennett's cap. It was good to see his brother smiling again. Just being at the cabin seemed to have that uplifting effect on him. On all of them. Even Lia had smiled at lunch, and it had made him want to see her smile even more.

"Well, I had an extra one I was going to give to you, but you can forget that." He pulled one from his back pocket. "Would you like it, Lia?"

Haydn turned to see Lia standing in the hallway a few feet from him. She'd changed into a blue soft-cotton T-shirt with a long black windbreaker loosely zipped to just above her navel, and cutoff denim shorts that sucked all the oxygen from the room. He couldn't breathe. Could. Not.

He forced himself to look back up at her face. *Don't be a creep, Haydn.* Why did he have to keep saying that to himself?

"Like what?" she asked Bennett, stepping closer to them.

"One of my fashion-forward hats."

Haydn groaned and attempted to steal the hat from Bennett's outstretched hand, but he dodged out of the way. "Don't torture her like this, Ben."

"Have some dignity, man." Jules folded his arms in a way

that showcased his muscles for Lia, and it took everything in Haydn not to roll his eyes. Or take him out at the knees.

Apparently, Haydn wasn't the only one feeling a spark of attraction for Lia. A spark? More like a roaring fire, but it wasn't out of control. Not yet.

"I love it." Lia put the hat on without hesitation. And it spoke to her solid beauty that the garishly colored bucket hat didn't diminish it one bit. In fact, the neon green added a healthy glow to her face.

Bennett lit up when she pulled the tie tight under her chin, and Haydn could have pulled Lia into a huge hug when he saw his brother's pleased expression. A hug of gratitude—and nothing else—of course. But he didn't want Jules to take *him* out at the knee, either.

Jules's scowl was back as he stepped in front of Lia before she could go outside. "Do you have any hiking boots?"

"No." She glanced down at her tennis shoes. "I hadn't really planned on hiking."

"You came to Alaska and didn't plan to hike?"

"Not everyone likes the outdoors," Haydn reminded Jules.

"I love the outdoors," Lia said defensively. "I packed in a hurry and didn't think about what I'd do once I got here."

"You'll be fine," Jules said, though his tone was doubtful enough to not inspire any confidence. "Should we go before that rain comes back?"

Haydn hesitated. He knew from dealing with Rosie that it was always a bad idea to comment on a woman's clothing choices, but he still asked, "Do you want to change into pants?"

She looked down at her shorts. "What's wrong with these?"

"Nothing." He swallowed. Hard. "It's just there are some pretty gnarly branches out there, and I don't want you to get caught on anything."

"I only brought leggings and shorts—and I have a feeling my leggings won't offer much more protection than these. But thanks for watching out for me." She shot a nervous glance at his camera, and he wondered if she was one of those girls who hated having their picture taken.

"Stay behind me, and I'll clear a path for you if things get too rough."

She smiled, and her face glowed even more. "Thank you, Haydn."

His chest puffed out like he was a character in one of those old cartoons. What was wrong with him? He was like a fly drawn to her Venus-y trap. A moth to her flame. A deer in her headlight. A human caught in her alien spaceship beam.

Whoa, that was some violent imagery he'd conjured up.

But he'd learned love only led to hurt. He'd seen how devastated his mom had been after his dad had left. He'd never want to feel that—or worse, make someone feel that way. And as long as this itch to keep moving crawled under his skin, as long as he couldn't be absolutely sure he'd wrestled it into submission, he'd never let himself fall for someone.

Even if her soft touch on his arm as she balanced herself to slide on her shoes made him feel as out of breath as climbing the West Rib on Denali. And as exhilarated.

He pushed the feeling aside, though his shoulders straightened with an undefinable sense of purpose as he led them into the forest, extremely aware of Lia right behind him.

9

LIA

The last time Lia had gone on a hike was immortalized forever in *Hot Goss Magazine*, after winning her first Grammy, because her childhood best friend had sold a picture of her to them. In it, Lia was a red-faced and sweaty teenager. She'd rolled her sleeves up, so they were like two bulky caterpillars near her neck, and she'd worn her favorite pair of leggings—black with neon-colored geometric shapes. Her best friend had braided her hair into a thick, frizzy French braid, and her braces-filled smile made Lia ache at the innocence of it all.

The worst part hadn't been everyone poking fun at the awkward stage of this younger, teenage Lia—though that had stung. It hadn't even been the betrayal of her old friend, and how used she'd felt. No, the worst part was realizing how badly she'd wanted that time in her life to remain untouchable, apart from the fame bubble her life had become.

But *nothing* was untouchable.

"Ope, be careful there," Bennett said, snagging her elbow as her shoes slipped over a moss-covered rock. "This stuff gets real slippery when wet."

Haydn paused and waited for them to catch up. He'd remained true to his word to hold back the thick, leafy branches when they cut into the dirt path, and so far, she'd managed not to get any scrapes. She'd also managed to take in Haydn's strong legs and back for the last thirty minutes.

Hiking in the misty rain wasn't so bad. She was definitely cold—her windbreaker was more for looks than for utility—but she wasn't going to complain. She'd only planned on hiding out from the world, eating, and singing sad songs. It sounded pathetic, especially now that she was out exploring her own private island with three handsome, outdoorsy men.

Though one man in particular kept catching her interest and holding it as tight as she'd held on to those plane armrests. She wasn't in the headspace for any sort of relationship, and maybe she'd never be, but she could appreciate a fine-looking and kind man in the same way she appreciated a stunning song or a breathtaking sunrise. And if songs or sunrises never made her feel like soda bubbles were fizzing through her veins the same way looking at Haydn did, well ... it wasn't like this was permanent. The rain would pass, they would leave—or she would, depending on if Jules got his way or not—and they'd all move on with their lives.

Haydn was clearly at home out here in the forest, walking a path that she couldn't pick out in the moss and plant overgrowth, but he confidently strode forward. His shoulders filled out his jacket nicely. Almost as nicely as his backside filled out his pants.

Bennett gave her a knowing smirk and nudged his elbow into her side teasingly.

"Sorry," she mouthed.

"Why are you sorry?" he said in a low voice as he shimmied his shoulders. "He's single, and you're his type."

"His type?" Why did she care? She was a lot of men's type— blonde, leggy, and gorgeous. She knew it wasn't misplaced confidence to say that. In her world, you had to be good-looking to make it.

"Spunky and spirited," he said, surprising her. It was hard to see herself as those things anymore, and not just a person who ran away when things got hard. "What's your type?"

"I'm not looking," she said as lightly as she could. "Just came off of a bad breakup."

"Me too." Bennett stuffed his hands in his pockets. "I proposed, and she broke up with me."

"Ouch." Lia gave in to the impulse to take his arm and give it a gentle hug. Something about Bennett—about all the Forrester brothers—made her feel safe. Like she could give them a piece of her without them trying to take everything. "I know we just met, but you've been wonderful. This feels like her loss."

He sighed and used his free hand to pat her arm. "Yeah. I guess. What about you? I can't imagine anyone breaking up with you."

"Well, you don't know me well enough yet, then." Her eyes stung, recalling how Bo had accused her of always placing him second behind her music. She pulled away from Bennett, needing to put some distance between them and his comfort. Bennett reminded her of a teddy bear, and it would be too easy to let down her guard with him. With all of them.

"I know you well enough," he said, in a tone that brooked no arguments and warmed her insides despite herself.

Thick pine trees towered overhead, and the sun was covered by both clouds and leaves, creating a misty, overcast atmosphere. Her mind spun with an eerie melody, and she hummed out a few notes. Her fingers itched to pick them out on her guitar. It sounded different than her usual upbeat pop songs, but for the first time in weeks, a tiny spark of creativity flared.

Haydn turned around to face her, every part of him radiating excitement. "The cabin is getting close."

"How many times have you been out here?" she asked.

"Dozens," Bennett answered, exasperated.

"Hundreds," Jules said, drawing out each syllable to sound like its own word.

"Not enough," Haydn countered. "I don't know why I think it's so cool. It just is."

"Is it haunted?" she asked teasingly.

"Probably." He rubbed his hands together, while the other two groaned.

"Don't get him started," Bennett pleaded with her.

"Too late," Jules grumbled. "He already rubbed his hands together like an evil villain."

Bennett shook his head. "Villainous monologue starting in three ... two ... one ..."

Haydn ignored them. "In the 1920s, a family moved from Pennsylvania to Alaska and built this cabin in the middle of nowhere."

"I cannot hear this story again," Bennett interrupted to say. "I'm going to take the shortcut to the cabin and meet you there."

"Yep," Jules agreed. "He's worse than a defense attorney grandstanding for the jury."

"Good luck, Lia." Bennett waved goodbye as he and Jules cut off into the forest, where the leaves and trees swallowed them up in seconds.

"Shortcut?" she asked.

"Yeah, but ..." He looked down at her legs, lingering just a beat longer than necessary. It took everything in her not to flex her calves. As if realizing he'd been caught checking her out, he raised his gaze to her face quickly, his cheeks a little redder than before. He cleared his throat. "Your legs will get chewed up by thorns on it."

She winced. "Yeah, that doesn't sound pleasant."

He shrugged. "I like this path better anyway, because two people can walk side by side for a lot of it."

She'd been walking beside Bennett for most of the hike because he made her feel the least unstable. She had her guard up with Jules, and Haydn had a way of smiling at her that stirred up emotions inside of her she wasn't quite ready to feel yet. And if their hands accidentally touched—well, she wanted that a little too much for her own peace of mind. Besides, the view from behind had been too good to give up.

"So what's the story?" she said to distract herself from the fact that she could feel the warmth radiating off his arm. What was it about him that drew her to him so fully? She liked watching those reality dating shows, and the couples always bonded after a high-adrenaline activity. So maybe that was it: they'd bonded after their turbulent flight. The thought put her at ease, and she was able to relax a bit. It made sense. It was human nature. And it wasn't like he was making any moves on her—appreciating her legs aside. And hadn't she just been appreciating his?

She could handle a mutual appreciation of legs.

"You sure you want to hear it?" Haydn asked with a raised eyebrow. He had a shadow of scruff on his chin and cheeks that contrasted with the boyish gleam in his eye.

"The suspense is killing me." She jokingly jumped from foot to foot like a child who can't contain their anticipation. He chuckled, and she loved the sound of it. Deep and throaty, like he was accustomed to laughing. Like it came easy to him.

"Okay, I'll start at the beginning. At least the beginning I know ... the family arriving on the island."

Haydn wove a story about a husband and wife with two young children who came to Alaska from Pennsylvania for adventure. "Travel journals were big business in the late 1800s and early 1900s, and many of them painted a romantic view of the Alaskan wilderness. This family followed the siren call of the northwest. That first summer they were here was a harsh one, followed by an even harsher winter. People in town saw the family less and less, until spring came and no one saw them at all.

"After the winter snow melted, someone came out here to check on them, and the only person who remained was the husband, half dead and mostly frozen. No one knew where his family had gone, not even him. If they'd moved to a different part of Alaska, *someone* surely would have heard something. Maybe they'd gone back to Pennsylvania because the adventure proved to be too much ..."

"Or maybe they didn't survive at all," Lia said quietly.

Haydn took her arm as she slipped on a particularly mossy rock, and she shivered. Whether from his touch or the story, she didn't know.

"The searchers brought the father to Winterhaven, but he escaped to return to the island only a few days later, nearly mad with his efforts. People in town soon began to see a murky yellow light out here at night, when the sky was darkest—no moon, mist covering the stars. No one ever saw him again. To this day, people still see that light on the darkest nights and say that it's that man, searching for his family."

She frowned. "That's really sad. Have you seen the light?"

He shook his head. "Rosie swears she has. I heard the story from a friend when we moved here, and when the island came up for sale, I convinced my brothers to go in on it with me and buy it."

"Why not Rosie too?"

"She was a teenager when we signed the papers. But she loves this place as much as the rest of us—if not more." He helped her navigate through some particularly thorny bushes, his hand firm around hers. "I'd noticed the last few times we came that sometimes things were moved or missing, and I figured it was her coming to stay without telling us—not that she was renting it out." He shook his head, but he smiled like he couldn't help being proud of her.

Haydn used a stick to hold back a huge patch of leaves that were bigger than her head and almost reached to her shoulder, revealing the cabin. It was small—no bigger than the bedroom she was sleeping in back at the cabin—and dilapidated. Rotted wooden slats framed smashed-in windows, and the roof sank downward like a limp sun hat.

The eerie melody flowed through her mind again, this time with a few extra notes. She hummed it, playing with the sound until it sounded exactly how she imagined it.

"What song is that?" Haydn said.

She had to be careful. If he started to associate her with music, he might guess who she was. "Just random notes. Like doodling, but with chords."

"Hmm. I can't relate. My doodling—both in song form and written—is terrible."

Bennett and Jules had already arrived and were leaning against a huge boulder while chatting. With both of them posed with their arms folded and legs crossed in an identical way, it was easy to see how much they looked alike.

She turned back to the cabin, a thrill zinging through her at the sight. The thick canopy of trees hung overhead, turning the steadily falling rain into a mist that hovered around them. It was like stepping into another world, one she hadn't even known existed, so far removed from her own it was like being in another universe.

Haydn had pulled out his camera and was taking pictures of the cabin, pausing to look through his viewfinder now and again.

"Don't you have enough pictures of that cabin yet?" Jules called out.

"I can't ever have enough," he replied. Lia wished she could relax at the sight of the camera. He was keeping it focused on the cabin, and nowhere near her. "I'm thinking about pitching a feature on the island for the magazine." He knelt to take a photograph from a different angle.

"It's about time," Jules said. "Are you going to tell the ghost story?"

"I think so." Haydn shrugged. "I haven't even run it by my editor yet. He might say no."

"Then send it to someone else. Like *Nature*," Bennett said.

Haydn's shoulders stiffened, something she might not have even noticed if she wasn't spending so much time checking out those shoulders. "Um, yeah. I guess I could do that," he said in a way that convinced no one that he was actually considering it.

Bennett's eyes narrowed, but before he could reply, Haydn turned to Lia. "Want to see inside?"

Excitement buzzed through her. This was better on so many levels than the pity party she'd planned for herself. "Can I?"

"Yes, just be careful where you step. There's a rotted-out porch, and the wood is questionable in some places."

She followed him up the stairs and through the open, hinged doorway of the cabin. Inside, it smelled musty and earthy. A rocking chair sat in the corner, and bones of some kind were nestled beneath it. "Please tell me that's an animal's bones."

"Critters like to bring their lunch in here." Haydn crouched down beside the bones. "Looks like something small. A bird of some sort. A raven, maybe."

She crouched beside him, feeling the closeness of him all along the side of her as she studied the bones and spotted a beak. He took a few pictures close up of the bones, and she looked over his shoulder to see how he was framing them.

The forgotten bones of who I used to be ...

"More doodling?" Haydn teased.

She hadn't even realized she'd started humming again. "I think in music," she said. "And apparently, I think out loud."

"I do my thinking through the lens, which might explain a lot. Two-dimensional, not very interesting thoughts ..."

She laughed. "Not true. You're a big deal. Remember that."

"How could I forget?"

"Do you have any magazines back at the cabin? I'd love to see your work."

"I do. But whatever you're expecting based on what my brothers have said, lower the bar to where limbo would be impossible."

"Well, I happen to be an expert at limbo. I can go super low."

They both paused a beat.

She groaned while he laughed. "That was weird. Let's pretend I didn't say that."

"Can't. Already pictured it."

"What happens at the cabin stays at the cabin," she said in a warning tone, but she knew the smile she couldn't hold back took out any actual weight in her words.

Still, Haydn held up his hand to his side. "Your limbo secrets are safe with me."

She pushed at his chest playfully. "Never say 'limbo secrets' again."

He shook his head regretfully. "That is a promise I'm unwilling to make."

She snorted out a laugh and then covered her mouth as if that could undo the sound. Her stomach twisted. She could just imagine that ugly laugh becoming a sound bite all over social media.

Haydn pulled her arm down gently. "Why are you hiding?"

"I just ... I have to be careful, Haydn."

"About what?"

"That laugh—I snorted. I don't do that."

"Why not? Everyone has a snort-laugh inside of them," he said, like it was no big deal.

She let out a small huff. "It's hard to explain, but my image is very important."

"These bones don't care what you laugh like. My brothers don't care." He leaned close to her, bringing with him the scent of his coconut sunscreen. "And I *like* your snort-laugh. It felt real."

It had been real, and that was the problem. It made her feel vulnerable in a way that opened her up to hurt, and she didn't want to hurt again. As he stared at her, the air between them thickened and seemed to vibrate with some sort of palpable magic. Like a flower drawn to sunlight, she found herself leaning closer to him.

"Ready to head back?" Jules's voice thundered through the cabin, and Lia tried not to notice how quickly Haydn sprang away from her and to his feet. Lia got to her feet more slowly, watching as Haydn busied himself with tucking his camera back into the case and definitely not looking her in the eye.

Interesting. She was not accustomed to men springing away from her like that. But it was definitely for the best. Whatever haze had sat between them dispersed into the air of the cabin, and now that she could think clearer, she was glad that Jules had interrupted before anything had happened.

Mostly glad.

She could not jump into another relationship so soon after Bo. She didn't want to. And even if she did want to, it wouldn't be fair to Haydn, though he was doing an excellent job of keeping a significant distance—an entire cabin's distance—between them. She didn't want to get hurt. She didn't want to hurt him. It was all good.

Mostly good.

She walked past Jules, who eyed her carefully, and onto the front porch. She glanced behind her to make sure Haydn was coming too—and, okay, to drink in the sight of him one last time before she really, truly put a stop to this growing ... bonding turbulent plane thing, or whatever it was she was feeling for him.

Which was her first mistake.

Her second? Forgetting Haydn's earlier warning.

Because while Lia was distracted by Haydn's perfectly kissable jawline, her foot hit a rotted plank on the porch that gave way and dumped her right into a thorny patch of devil's club.

10

HAYDN

*H*aydn directed Lia to sit on the sofa while he retrieved the first-aid kit from the bathroom. She'd handled falling in devil's club like a champ, but he knew there were still thorns in her, and cuts that needed to be cleaned out and disinfected.

When Lia had fallen, all thoughts of nearly kissing her had flown from his mind. Well, maybe not flown, but at least landed in a tree branch somewhere to wait out the crisis at hand. What would have happened if Jules hadn't walked in right then?

He both wanted to think about it nonstop and never think of it again.

Haydn had rushed to Lia, getting to her just after Jules had hauled her out of the porch and into his arms. Jealousy had writhed in Haydn as Jules carried her off the porch and through the thick patch of thorny weeds before gently setting her down on the rock he and Bennett had been sitting on.

If Haydn hadn't been avoiding her so intensely, he could have stopped her from falling. Or at least been close enough to be the one to carry her instead of Jules. What was wrong with him? Being around Lia was muddling his brain worse than the lack of oxygen had on Denali.

"I remember the first time I fell into a devil's club patch," Bennett was saying as Haydn returned from the hall closet with the kit. Lia sat beside Bennett, her legs propped up on the coffee table Haydn had pulled up close for her. Jules put some popcorn in the microwave, which filled the house with a delicious, buttery popcorn scent, and put water in the kettle for more hot chocolate. None of them liked feeling helpless, and seeing Lia hurt was doing exactly that and leading to a general sense of restlessness between them.

Lia was shaking with cold when Haydn knelt in front of her, and goose bumps had risen on her arms and legs. He snagged the plush buffalo-plaid blanket she'd been using earlier and wrapped it snugly around her shoulders. Her fingers brushed his, and they were like ice. It had gotten colder and wetter as they'd walked back to the house, and they'd gone slower to accommodate for the pain in her legs, so her heart rate hadn't risen high enough to keep her warm.

"Where did you get this blanket?" she asked through chattering teeth as she snuggled into the blanket. The red on the fabric nearly matched the redness on her cheeks and lips. He wanted to hold her face in his hands and warm it up, but he didn't know if she'd welcome his touch or not—and either reaction made his stomach twist uncomfortably. "It's the softest blanket ever."

"At a thrift shop in Wrangell. The label was torn out, so we have no idea what brand it is. Rosie would love to know too. She's tried to steal it a few times."

"I don't blame her." She rubbed her cheek against it, and a flare of heat shot through Haydn, imagining that cheek rubbing his own. Yeah, he'd definitely want her to welcome his touch.

"I'm going to take a look at your legs," he said, his voice a little too gruff.

Bennett raised a knowing eyebrow. *So, you are attracted to her.* As Irish twins that sometimes felt like full twins, Haydn could read Bennett's looks just as easily as his texts.

Of course I am, loser, he glared in return. *Don't be annoying about it.*

Bennett folded his arms loosely in a sort of gloating satisfaction. Yes, Haydn wanted to cheer his brother up this week, but that didn't mean he wanted Bennett all up in his business to do it.

He ran his hand lightly over her leg to feel for thorns he couldn't see, and heard Lia catch her breath. "Have you done this before?" she asked.

"Yes," he said. "I'm EMT trained, and it comes in handy when I'm out exploring." He couldn't call an ambulance out to a mountain peak, so he made sure he had the knowledge to help, and it had been essential and lifesaving more than once.

"Interesting." She swallowed hard as his hand slid under her knee to the soft skin there, where, thankfully, he felt no evidence of thorns.

Scratches covered the length of Lia's long legs, most of them superficial, but there were a few deep enough to require butterfly bandages. She had several thick, deep thorns stuck in her calves and ankles, and he used the tweezers to pull them out while Bennett regaled her with stories of fishing trips gone wrong.

"Maybe you need to make a weight minimum for fishers?" she suggested, laughing at yet another story of someone falling overboard while attempting to reel in a fish. She winced as Haydn pulled out another thorn. He'd had to remove ten so far.

"Sorry," he murmured. "Almost done."

"It happens to all sizes!" Bennett said, laughing as well. "I've had the tiniest customers pulling up fish twice their size, while a former linebacker once got yanked into the ocean."

Lia settled deeper into the couch as Jules handed her a mug with raspberry hot chocolate. She placed her face over the steaming brim of the cup and inhaled deeply. "That smells like dessert," she told him. "Thank you. I can't believe I'm requiring so much care." She scrunched up her nose as if disappointed in herself.

"Yes, you're so difficult," Jules deadpanned.

Lia was caught somewhere between an apologetic smile and a frown.

"He's joking," Bennett whispered. If Lia's fall could have any positive benefit at all, it was that Jules had softened toward her considerably because of it.

Haydn ran the pads of his fingers over her calf and shin to check for any more thorns he might have missed, and her skin was softer than that blanket she was snuggled in. Goose bumps popped up along her skin following his touch, making his heart skip a beat.

"No more thorns here." He cleared his throat. "Let's do the other leg."

He made quick work of finishing his task, forcing his mind to focus on the cuts and scrapes and not the woman who these legs belonged to. When that didn't work, he mentally recited as many species of plant indigenous to Alaska as he could recall.

While Haydn was distracting himself from being distracted by Lia's legs—see? He was all discombobulated—Jules had handed out bowls of popcorn to everyone. Haydn hopped up, relieved and disappointed when Lia tucked her legs under the blanket.

"Yours is on the counter," Jules said.

Haydn put the first-aid kit away and washed his hands before taking his food and hot chocolate into the living room.

Bennett was telling another story about a fighting couple who decided to get a divorce in the first hour of an eight-hour boat trip. Bennett could always be counted on to have the best stories. Haydn was used to being alone and reveling in the quiet when he was out photographing new locations. He didn't mind it—not much, anyway. But being in this cozy, warm room with his brothers and Lia, talking and laughing, made him realize how lonely it could get out there.

"I can't imagine anything more awkward," Lia said through fingers that covered her mouth in horror. Her eyes were alight with humor that dispelled some of the sadness that always seemed to linger on her face even when she smiled.

"Seven hours of a pendulum swinging between ignoring each other and screaming every grievance they had. Then they only caught one fish, and they were yelling about who was going to get custody of it in the settlement—even though I kept assuring them I could cut it into equal halves. I felt like Solomon."

Her eyes were watery with tears of laughter. "Stop. You're totally making this up."

He held up his fingers in the scout salute. "I swear I'm not. If I've learned one thing in my job, it's that people are weird and unexplainable."

She took a sip of her hot chocolate, looking contemplative. "You know, you're absolutely right."

"Except for us, of course," Haydn assured her, wanting her to look his way again, wanting her to smile at him like that and hear her snort-laugh again. "We're just three normal blokes." Blokes? Was he British now? *Yep, way to prove you're normal.* It was too much to hope his brothers could let that one go.

"Right-o, mate," Jules replied in an accent. "Doesn't get more normal than us."

"Blimey, after a proper cuppa, we're just grand," Bennett added. He held out his mug toward Jules, who tapped his mug against it with his pinkie held aloft.

Haydn rubbed his temples. So much for playing it cool. Out in the wild, people respected him and looked to him for his leadership. They'd never mock him like this. That's what he got for having two brothers. If he acted as defensive as he felt, they'd never let it go. Which meant he had to lean in.

"I'm trying to assure Lia that we're not ... dodgy." He gave the last word the most Oliver-Twisty accent he could muster.

His brothers howled, and Lia's eyes glowed as brightly as the fire as she watched them all.

"On that note ..." She set her mug on the table and stood, clutching the blanket around her shoulders. "I'm going to get ready for bed." She gave Haydn a mischievous smile. "I'm feeling absolutely knackered." Her accent sounded so real, Haydn wouldn't have been surprised to learn she'd spent a significant amount of time in Europe.

Bennett and Jules chuckled while Haydn shook his head in defeat. "Fine, fine. You all win. Especially Lia. Did you grow up in England?"

She gave him one of her unreadable smiles that made him want to sit and talk with her for hours and find out all of her secrets. "I've spent some time there."

He wanted to ask more, get her to stay with them, to keep joking around and telling stories and learn more about her, but she yawned into the blanket. "Do you mind if I use the hallway bathroom for a quick shower?" she asked.

"It's yours," Bennett assured her. "We can use the bathroom in Jules's room if we need to."

"Thank you." She paused. Was it Haydn's imagination, or did her gaze linger on him extra long before she left?

The room felt too quiet once she was in the bathroom. She'd brought a vibrancy to the group, and now that it was missing, he wished to have it back.

The sound of her humming drifted out to them, that same

tune she'd been thinking out loud to at the cabin, and then the sound of the shower turned on and drowned it out.

"You think she's gorgeous," Bennett said in a singsong voice.

"You want to kiss her," Jules said.

"You want to—"

Haydn threw a pillow at Bennett's face before he could finish. "Stop," he moaned.

"Too late. That one's an earworm," Jules told him.

"All Rosie's movie quotes are," Bennett agreed, "but I find them appropriate for most occasions."

"Well, I did have to promise Rosie we'd watch two more romantic comedies next time we're all together," Haydn said. "To make up for the cabin thing."

"Make up for it?" Jules sat up straighter. "She's the one who—"

"I know."

"And it's not our fault that—"

"I *know*."

"And if she thinks—"

"She does. And we will."

Jules let out a disgruntled huff but dropped the issue. To be honest, none of them hated the movies, and all three of them knew they'd done Rosie wrong by leaving her out of so many of their trips. Without their dad around, they were the only steady males she had in her life.

He'd successfully distracted his brothers from pushing him to talk about Lia, but that didn't mean he wasn't thinking of her. He did like her. He hadn't been so intrigued by any woman— ever.

And yes, she was gorgeous in the way where he almost needed to blink to assure himself that she really did exist. Especially on this island, where myths were bigger than reality.

It was more than her stunning good looks, though, that drew him in. It was the way she hummed notes like they belonged in the air they flowed into, the adventurous spark in her mysterious eyes, how she made Bennett smile again and Jules soften and Haydn want to unfurl his roots into the dark Alaskan soil.

It was dangerous, this new dynamic she brought. And it couldn't last.

11

LIA

*L*ia stepped out of the shower to hear the low rumble of the brothers' voices drifting down the hallway. She couldn't make out what they were saying, but the happy sound of it was comforting. Lia lived alone, and even though she'd convinced herself that she liked it that way, she missed the sound of someone else in the house, existing in her sphere, adding their own energy to her space.

Ideas lit up in her mind like an old-school switchboard, each one demanding her attention before another one lit up just as quickly. She changed into a fresh pair of leggings and a tank top before throwing on an off-the-shoulder, oversized tour sweatshirt. Gathering her things, she took one last look at herself in the steamy mirror—pink cheeked, wet haired, and for once not feeling like all she wanted to do was cry.

When she'd discovered Bo's and Gwen's relationship, she'd been devastated but still felt like she had her feet beneath her. When she'd learned they'd stolen her songs and recorded them behind her back, it was a bit like how it felt to fall through the floor at the cabin: one moment steady and absolutely confident in her support, and the next careening downward into a patch of painful thorns.

The worst part was that her muse had tucked tail and fled, and she'd been unable to coax it back. Not even sure if she wanted to try. Some people wrote from a place of pain. They fed off of those emotions to create and heal.

Not Lia.

Though she included her painful experiences in her writing, she needed to write from a place of joy. Or at least acceptance. Her devastation led to nothing but blank pages and un-plucked strings as her mind whirled over everything she must have missed for those two to betray her so terribly for so long. And so easily.

Maybe that was the most difficult part of it all—she'd been so trusting, she'd never once suspected anything until her manager had send her Gwen's latest demo and she'd recognized the song right away. From there, it was like a house of cards falling, one truth coming out after another.

How gullible she'd been.

But she didn't want to think about them anymore.

Instead, she rushed to her room and riffled around her duffel bag for the pen and paper she almost hadn't brought with her. She wished she had her guitar, but she'd left it in the living room. She was already infringing on the brothers' house; she didn't want to impose on more of their brotherly time, no matter how much they insisted they didn't mind.

And she didn't think she'd have the restraint to go in, grab her guitar, and leave them again. Not if Bennett started another story, not if Jules had another drink for her, and definitely not if Haydn motioned for her to sit beside him, giving her a tingling feeling throughout her entire body with one look.

She opened the notebook decisively to jot down some of the images she'd seen that afternoon.

Light-dappled dust in a forgotten place.

Thorns hidden under soft leaves.

Lost love.

She wrote out as many words as she could, and started linking phrases together. Hours passed, but it felt like only minutes, and it was only when the boys stopped talking that she realized their quiet chatter had been the peaceful backdrop to her songwriting session.

She heard them moving around in the hall and bathroom, then heading into the bedrooms. She ached to pick up the guitar and pluck out the notes she'd been humming earlier, along with some of the lyrics she'd pulled together, but she didn't want to keep any of them up.

Instead, she got into bed. Haydn's bed.

She tried not to think of him, but it was impossible when the bed smelled just like him. His sheets were soft and smooth against her skin, not unlike how his hand had felt running down her leg so tenderly, yet so capably, as he'd taken care of her thorns. In some ways, he seemed like a remnant from another century. She'd never met anyone quite like Haydn.

She finally gave in to the urge to burrow her face into Haydn's pillow and breathe in his scent. Forest and sunshine. The undeniable essence of him.

She reached for her notebook and wrote the words down, then a few more descriptors of Haydn. She was not writing a song about him. Nope. She'd written one about Bo, and look where that'd gotten her.

To prove it to herself, she also wrote down a phrase about Bennett: sad smiles meet sunny stories. And for Jules: rigid lines hide softness inside. There.

All noises had quieted down, and it seemed that everyone was asleep. She lay there for another hour, her brain unable to stop racing through new lyrics about the cabin and the Forrester brothers, especially Haydn. Smelling his pillow and knowing he'd been in this bed before wasn't helping anything.

Lia accepted the reality that she was not going to sleep until she figured this song out.

She opened the bedroom door and peered into the hall. Every light was off. A dim grayish glow from the setting sun still filtered in through the floor-to-ceiling windowed wall of the cabin. She could hear the calming crash of waves on the shore, the pulsing rush of wind rustling through the trees, and the steady patter of rain on the roof, but otherwise, all was still and silent.

She found her guitar case where she'd left it in the living room, sat on the couch with it on her lap, and pulled her guitar out. She ran her hand along the length of the rosewood body. She'd had this guitar since her first album's royalty payment. She'd spent nearly the entire amount to buy this guitar, and she rarely let it out of her sight.

She clipped on the guitar silencer and ran her fingers over the strings, eliciting the softest of sounds in the vibrations. It was like coming home.

That should be quiet enough. She played a few chords until she got the right one. The one she'd been humming all day. There. All her tension from the last month released in one strum. She sighed in satisfaction.

It had been so long since she'd felt this inspired. One day here without drama, without her phone, without people making her feel horrible, and the music was coming back again. It felt good. Right.

In a way things hadn't felt right in a very long time.

12

HAYDN

*B*ennett's bed was too soft. Haydn rolled toward the edge of it, away from Bennett—who slept with his mouth open and snored, ugh—but it was like swimming through moss. Impossible and suffocating.

Since Haydn hadn't planned on sharing a bed with his brother, he hadn't brought his earplugs, like he might have if they'd gone on a camping trip. He tried to wrap the pillow around his head to muffle the sound of his brother's breathing, but it wasn't quite big enough to cover both ears.

With a frustrated huff, he extricated himself from the morass of a bed without waking Bennett. He threw the pillow on the ground and lay down, but that was worse. They hadn't gotten around to getting rugs for the bedrooms yet, and the floor was hard and cold and gritty with sand against his bare shoulder.

He rolled onto his back and stared at the ceiling.

He could spend the night dreaming he was being suffocated by a ton of cotton balls. He could spend the night accepting the pain the floor deemed to inflict upon him.

Or he could sleep on the couch.

Done.

He opened the door quietly and tiptoed into the hallway. Bennett kept up a happy face all day, but he'd struggled to fall asleep, and Haydn knew it was because he was thinking of his ex. And Jules was the lightest sleeper on the planet, which was in part why Haydn had chosen to share with Bennett and not sleep in Jules's larger bed.

And also because Jules basically slept on a board because it was supposedly good for his back. And Haydn had no confidence his brother wouldn't have accidentally-on-purpose kidney-kicked him in the middle of the night.

Haydn walked toward the living room, but paused when he heard music. Guitar. It started and stopped again, and the only indication he had that he wasn't listening to a recording was the sound of chords playing then changing and then pencil scribbling.

He walked to the open doorway of the living room and leaned his shoulder against the wall.

Lia sat on the couch, her blonde hair long and wavy down over her slender shoulders and down her back, which was bent over her guitar. A pencil stuck out of the side of her mouth, and she played a few notes, then pulled the pencil out, wrote a few things down, and stuck it back in her mouth again.

When she turned to her guitar, he could see her profile. Her face was creased in concentration, and one word flitted through his mind. Cute. She looked cute sitting there, intently working on a song, her concentration solely on what she was doing. Again, that sense that he'd seen her somewhere before nudged him, but he couldn't place where that possibly might have been.

He didn't want to startle her, but he also didn't want to continue to stand here, watching her without her knowing. He was totally and completely captivated by her, and she was clearly in the middle of an intense train of thought. He didn't want to ruin that.

She gathered her hair into her hand and pulled it over her shoulder, revealing a bare shoulder that arrested his attention. Then she began to sing, her voice low and husky and sexy in all the best ways, and he was completely nailed in place.

Lia was good. Really good. She looked at home with her guitar, like it was a natural extension of her body. She stopped playing and took the pencil from behind her ear to jot something down, then set it on the couch beside her. This was the most relaxed he'd seen her, and he didn't want to interrupt it.

And he'd been standing here long enough that he'd probably crossed the line from admiring and straight into stalker territory. He should slip back to Bennett's room and leave Lia alone.

He moved to take a step back, but his heel got caught on the corner of the side table, and it squealed across the floors like a bald eagle's call.

She jumped with a squeak and whirled toward him. "Haydn!" She placed a hand over her heart as if doing so would still it. Her eyes flickered to his bare chest for the quickest of instances, and since he was human, he flexed. He wasn't proud of it, but he did it. "You scared me. Did I wake you up?"

She yawned, and the comfortable sight of it was disarming enough to make him feel tongue tied. Had he ever felt this way about a woman before? No, he definitely had not.

"Haydn?" she asked, sounding unsure.

He cleared his throat as he sat down, still making sure to keep his stomach flexed like a teenage lifeguard at the pool. "No, you didn't wake me up," he replied, trying to sound normal. Calm, cool, and collected. Was his voice pitched lower than usual? "Bennett's bed is horrible, and I don't know how he sleeps on that thing, so I came out here to maybe sleep or at least read, and you're incredible."

Way to play it cool, *mate*. Boy, if there was any time he could use his brothers to act as a buffer between him and being awkward, it would be now.

She folded her arms over her sweatshirt and sank into the couch.

He winced. "I just mean ... yeah." He didn't know what he meant, except he wished she'd keep playing. He let his abs relax, because they were starting to burn, and she wasn't looking at him anyway. She was staring out the window, looking similar to how she had yesterday morning right before she'd fled for the boat. He hated seeing her look so uneasy.

"I'm sorry to eavesdrop," he continued when she didn't say anything. "I'm guessing playing and singing must be a really private thing for you."

She snort-laughed and then covered her mouth again, her eyes wide as she looked at him. "Stop making me do that," she said through her fingers.

He felt his shoulders relax slightly. "Nope. I won't promise that."

She shook her head and then dropped her hand to let her fingers rest on the guitar strings. It was too dark to clearly read the expression on her face, but he thought he saw deep sadness etched there.

"I won't tell anyone you sing. Patient-doctor confidentiality," he teased. It was a dumb joke, but it eased some of the tension he felt in the room.

"You did have to bandage me up earlier," she told him with a faint smile, merely an echo of her smiles from earlier.

"Exactly." He clasped his hands between his knees and stared at her seriously. He really wished he'd thought to grab a shirt before coming out here to sleep. "I know how to keep things private, Lia, if you ever want to talk." He'd always been a private person; that was part of what had drawn him toward nature photography—the music in the wilderness and expansive space to stretch out in. The endless nooks to explore. The vibrant colors and all the stories nature held. The draw to do that across the world tugged at him even stronger than before. It was getting harder to nudge that feeling aside.

Lia let out a shallow breath and nodded her head just once, like she believed him. "It's better. Being out here." She ran her fingers lightly over the guitar strings in a way that made his heart race. *Focus, Haydn.* "Away from it all."

"From your breakup?"

She raised an eyebrow at him.

"Bennett told us. He may not be as good at keeping things private as I am." Yeah, that'd convince her to open up. Why did he want her to open up in the first place? He didn't know, except he wanted to see some of the sadness lift from her eyes again, and sometimes talking through things helped.

"Noted," she said wryly. "And yes, the breakup. Along with my job and everyone who has opinions about how I'm living my life."

"Sounds stressful."

"It is. Being out here, though, it helps. Like the world is bigger than my best friend and my boyfriend getting together behind my back."

"Wait—seriously? That sucks."

"Yep. And they stole a bunch of my work and took credit for it." She turned toward him fully, and he felt her relaxing into his presence again.

"You all worked together too?"

She shook her head ruefully. "Unfortunately."

"There's got to be something you can do," he said, feeling fired up on her behalf. He never liked injustice, and it was coming against Lia, of all people. Lia, who was so kind and who made Bennett smile again and got Jules to chill out and ... He kind of wanted to punch something—her ex's face, maybe. He wasn't a violent person. He was more the zen nature type, so this was a new feeling for him. "Tell your boss what they did, or ... I don't know, let's set up a hidden recording to get them to admit they stole your work. I'll pose as an investor or something. I'm realizing I don't even know what you do, but we'll figure out a plan that works. I'm not sure if recording someone without their knowledge is breaking the law or not—but Jules can represent us if needed."

She smiled at him.

"What?"

"I just ... thank you for believing me."

"Of course I believe you."

"And being willing to break the law for me."

"I'm Alaskan. Laws are mere *suggestions* out here."

She laughed, and it felt more satisfying than having his first feature picked up by *Alaska Ridges Magazine*. Well, on the same level as that, at least. Especially now that he knew how much stress and sadness was weighing her down.

He rested his hand along the back of the couch, his fingers inches from her shoulder. It wouldn't take much to cross that small space, and yet he knew he shouldn't. "You should stay here at the cabin," he said. "I'll tell my brothers we have to go tomorrow. They'll listen to me."

"No." The light strumming paused, and her gaze again fell on his chest. It took every single ounce of self-discipline he possessed not to flex his abs again. She followed the line of his stomach, up his chest and then across his outstretched arm, her gaze like a touch on his skin. She looked back at the guitar strings, and he could breathe again. "This is your place, and I've overstayed my welcome as it is."

"That's not true."

She leveled him with a look. "You're right. I wasn't ever welcome in the first place."

"That's because we didn't know you. We know you now."

"Not well."

"Well enough." Haydn shook his head. "I'm going to be stubborn about this. You need the cabin this week more than we do."

"We're at an impasse, it seems." Her fingers picked up speed over the strings as they flowed on them like water over rocks on the stream by the cabin.

"What song is this?" he asked.

"A new one I'm working on," she told him. "Does this sound familiar?"

She started to sing, and he recognized the tune from earlier. Sometimes she had words—things about light and dust—but a lot of the time, she just hummed out a melody.

"And this one too," she said, jumping straight into another song, her voice a little louder and surer as she hummed through a different melody, a variation on the earlier one. It made him feel like he was back on the trail to the cabin, back in that very favorite place on earth to be—with her, in their own world.

Her eyes met his as she came to the end of the song, and a waterfall of emotion flowed over him, stealing his ability to breathe properly. Their gazes held, and he leaned closer, drawn to her by some force he couldn't understand. She leaned closer too, and her eyes fluttered shut. Her soft hand came to rest on his chest, igniting a fire in him, and this time, he gave in to the urge to flex his pecs.

Their lips were a mere whisper away from touching when one of the bedroom doors slammed against the wall. Lia's eyes flew open, and she dropped her hand quickly as she pulled away. Haydn slowly blinked, still caught in her spell, until an irritated, robe-clad Jules stalked into the room. Haydn couldn't see his scowl in the dim light, but he could feel it.

"For the love of all that is good in this world," he growled. "Would you two please stop talking and singing and playing music? I. Can't. Sleep."

Lia sucked in her lips, but before she could respond, Haydn turned fully toward his brother. "Maybe it's your rock-hard bed that's the problem."

"The bed is fine. You probably think you're talking quietly, Haydn, but you're not. Your low voice carries, and even if I can't hear what you're saying, I can hear *you*. Lia, you sound amazing, but please wait to play until morning," he pleaded, sounding a little less grumpy as he rubbed at his eyes. "If everyone will go to bed right now, we can all stay for the week. Problem solved. No more discussion needed. Good night." And with that, he turned on his heel and went back into his bedroom with a decisive door click behind him.

"O-kay," Lia said, carefully placing her guitar into its case.

"You don't have to listen to him. It's not just his house," Haydn spoke extra loud on purpose. "If you want to keep playing, go for it."

"That's okay. It's late. I should go to bed and leave the couch to you." She bit her bottom lip, and he gave in to the urge to tug it free with his thumb. Heat shot through him as she stared at him, and he yanked his hand away. What was he thinking? She'd just told him of her bad breakup, and it seemed like the right time to make a move? He was usually much better at reading a room than this.

Maybe he'd spent too much time in nature and was losing his touch. Lack of oxygen from climbing high peaks had killed too many brain cells. How else could he explain why he was drawn to her so fully when he had no space in his life for another person? "Yeah, of course."

"Good night," she whispered, her words a mere breath of air in the night, and then she disappeared down the hall and into his room.

Haydn lay awake on the couch long after she'd left, knowing that sleep would be eluding him for a while.

13

LIA

*L*ia pulled the drawstring of Haydn's sweatpants as tight as she could around her waist. The pant legs flooded around her ankles, but at least her legs would be protected from any devil's club for today's outing.

She walked out of the bedroom to find Haydn standing with his back to her, half leaning into the hallway's open closet. His shirt stretched tightly over his shoulders, revealing the muscles she got to see up close last night. When he'd walked into the living room without a shirt on. Wearing only low-slung pajama pants. His six-pack and muscled chest had made all coherent thoughts sputter straight out of her mind, like water attempting to shoot out of a kinked-up hose. Thinking about it now made her swallow against the dryness in her throat.

And that almost-kiss? She couldn't decide if she was relieved or disappointed that Jules had interrupted them.

The muscles in Haydn's T-shirt clad back tightened as he reached farther into the closet for something, and she barely refrained from sighing like a lovesick teenager. Disappointed. *Definitely* disappointed. Which meant it was a *really* good thing they'd been interrupted.

Haydn riffled through a bin resting on the floor, then stood, holding up a pair of brown boots that he studied from all angles. He was going to turn around and catch her watching him. She could already feel her cheeks heating up at the prospect, yet she couldn't give up this moment of observing him without him realizing it.

So many people put on a show around her, never revealing their true selves. It was rare that people interacted with her without knowing who she was, and gave her an unfiltered, unmoderated look at who they were.

They'd hardly spoken more than a couple of words since everyone had woken up. It turned out that Haydn was not a morning person—evidenced by his wildly sleep-mussed hair and adorably grumpy frown until he ate his breakfast—which his brothers teased him endlessly over.

But he had shared a sleepy smile with her that made her insides soar as if harnessed to an aerial lift, and then he'd tossed her a pair of his joggers before heading to the shower, which her bedroom shared a wall with. Well, Haydn's just-right bedroom that she was sleeping in. The shower water had turned on, which she didn't think about for one second. No sir. Instead, she'd played her guitar—and okay, fine, most of the lyrics were terribly pedestrian about brown eyes and long, finger-runnable hair and sideways smiles.

Speaking of sideways smiles ...

Haydn had spotted her watching him, and his distracted expression slid straight into a grin she felt all the way to the tips of her fingers. Fingers that very much wanted to press against that chest again. Or run through his dark, silky hair that had been washed and pulled back into a short knot at his nape.

"Well, I won't be featured on any magazine covers wearing these, but they should do the trick." She twirled as if she stood at the end of a runway in a designer gown. She caught the appreciative gleam in his eye as he chuckled.

"That's Alaska chic," he informed her.

"All you need is a black hoodie," Bennett said as he walked out of his room, slinging an empty duffel over his shoulder.

"And a worn-out cap," Jules said. He'd put on a pair of khaki pants that weren't creased, and his flannel, collared shirt was unbuttoned over a plain gray T-shirt. So he *could* relax a little.

"I've got my bucket hat," she said, pulling it from her day pack and stuffing it on her head.

Jules frowned while Bennett smiled. She hadn't actually been planning on wearing it, but she couldn't resist the double benefit of frustrating Jules while making Bennett happy. She'd only known these brothers for a couple of days, and already she wondered how Rosie juggled all their strong personalities.

Probably by doing whatever she wanted ... like putting their cabin up on a vacation rental site as a side hustle.

Today, they were going to explore some tide pools. An adventure that Lia was almost embarrassingly excited for. Lia hadn't had a vacation plan when she'd booked this trip to Alaska—her sole goal being to escape Nashville. If pressed, she might say that she planned to play her guitar—because why else would she have brought it?—and sleep as much as humanly possible. But the Forrester brothers were active and enthusiastic and knowledgeable about what the island had to offer—and, okay, they were hot too, but it wasn't *just* that—and suddenly, sleeping as much as humanly possible didn't seem nearly as appealing as it had a couple days ago.

Plus, the brothers were funny. She could watch them interact with each other all day long. Well, to be fair, she could watch Haydn do pretty much *anything* all day long.

"Try these boots on," Haydn told her. He held out a pair of brown rubber boots that would go nearly to her knee. "They're Rosie's."

She pulled them on over the thick pair of socks she'd found in Haydn's dresser, and they fit perfectly. She folded down the sides like Rosie had, to find these ones lined with silky material patterned with bright turquoise and yellow swirls.

She layered a sweater under her waterproof jacket this time, and re-fitted her lime-green "Forrester Expedition" bucket hat over her braids. By the time she met the brothers outside, the late-morning sun was already peeking through the clouds, offering pockets of warmth and light. A misty rain fell, something she was realizing was a staple on this island.

Haydn walked on one side of Lia, and Bennett on the other, while Jules led the three of them through the woods, like the Peter Pan to their Lost Boys, and then at a sharp angle toward the beach. She breathed in the fresh scent that she could only describe as green and leafy and would always associate with this island. A crackling sound filled the air around them, like air bubbles releasing from underwater.

"These are where the best tide pools are," Bennett informed her. He'd filled the duffel bag with snacks, and it crinkled as he positioned it from one shoulder to the other. "Over by the house isn't as good."

"Plus it's a longer walk," Jules chimed in over his shoulder, "so Haydn's blood gets pumping enough for him to be his bright, sunshiny self once again."

Haydn scowled.

"Longer!" Bennett shouted, holding his arm up as if he were holding a staff and waging a battle cry.

Lia giggled, and Haydn bumped his shoulder into hers. She looked up to find him leaning close, and he whispered, "Do you want to know a secret?"

"Very much," she whispered back.

His voice got a little louder. "It's not the mornings that make me grumpy. It's my annoying brothers."

"Hey!" Bennett said. "I made you scrambled eggs this morning."

"That were burned," Haydn pointed out.

"It's not my fault the book I was reading got so good that I forgot I was cooking."

"Whose fault is it, then?" Jules asked.

"The author's." Bennett shook his head dramatically. "They don't care if a meal gets ruined because I'm too invested in the story to know what's going on around me. It really is a shame."

The banter between them continued the rest of the way to shore. At some point, probably when Lia slipped and slid over some mossy rocks, Haydn reached out his hand, and she slid her palm against his. She hadn't been this excited to hold hands with someone since junior high. She resisted the urge to burrow into his side, barely, but she did love the steady feel of his arm pressed snugly against hers.

They exited the sandy tree line to find a long, beachy expanse of rough-edged barnacles, slimy rockweed, and dark green kelp, with pockets of colorful sea organisms.

The sun's bright rays fully shone on them here, and Lia reluctantly let go of Haydn's arm to unzip her rain jacket, and then pull off her sweater beneath it to tie around her waist.

Haydn pulled out his camera and started to take pictures, pausing between each one to mess around with buttons on his screen, before taking more.

"We could be here for hours," Jules said under his breath with a nod in Haydn's direction. He'd wandered farther away, deep enough into the water that it nearly came to the tops of his boots, as he captured a picture of another distant island.

"Well, shoot. I've got such a busy day ..." She grinned, and was gratified when one side of his mouth curved up just a bit. She could think through new songs here just as easily as she could back at the cabin. She'd brought a notebook and pencil in her day pack.

"There's a spot up that hill—" He pointed to a small hill about a quarter of a mile away. "—where we can sometimes get reception, if you want to check your phone."

She shuddered. That was the last thing she wanted to do. She hadn't even brought her phone with her this morning. "Okay," she told him. "I'm good for now, though."

They stood side by side, the air between them turning awkward. It seemed like he wanted to say something, and her stomach twisted at what it might be.

He knows who you are. He changed his mind about letting you stay. He hates your guts. Inner Gwen sounded way too delighted about that last one.

He made a ticking sound as he rocked back on his heels and stuck his hands in his pockets.

"Look, Jules—"

"Lia, I—"

They both stopped abruptly after talking over one another.

"You first," he insisted in a tone that brooked no arguments.

"I was just going to say that if it makes you too uncomfortable for me to be here, I can leave." She didn't know where she'd go, but that was hardly Jules's problem.

"No. I said you could stay, and I never go back on my word."

"Oh. Well, okay." She stared out at the horizon where Haydn stood, getting a close-up photograph of something in the water. Maybe one of the many colorful starfish dotting the beach like sprinkles on a vanilla cupcake.

"I wanted to talk about Haydn."

She tore her gaze away from Haydn to look at Jules, who stood with his arms folded. He had a serious expression—even more serious than usual, which was really saying something— directed right at her. She didn't know what kind of lawyer Jules was, but she could imagine him as a prosecutor, facing her as a witness on the stand for the defendant. Or maybe she *was* the defendant he believed was guilty.

Either way, she both wanted to squirm under his glare and hold her shoulders back to prove he couldn't get to her. Even if he very much was getting to her.

"Haydn puts a lot of pressure on himself. To take care of all of us."

"And he doesn't need one more person to care for," she finished. "I have no intention of—"

He interrupted with an abrupt shake of his head and said, "No, that's not what I was going to say at all."

"Oh." Maybe she'd just listen to what he had to say, then. She rocked back on her heels with her hands in her back pockets, curious to hear what he said now that she realized she wasn't being warned away from Haydn.

"He thinks that without him, we'd all fall apart. And we do rely on him a lot. It's hard not to when he's so willing to help."

He paused for long enough that she wondered if he was done, but he stood there, staring out at the horizon, so she held still, hoping there was more. She wasn't disappointed.

"But I think he's holding himself back because of us," he continued. "He thinks he's the glue, and without him we'll all fall apart."

She'd heard him refer to himself as the glue when he'd been talking to Rose. "Why does he think that?"

"It's something our dad used to say, before he left. Haydn doesn't invest himself in relationships other than with us or jobs that would take him out of Alaska."

Lia looked out to where Haydn was chatting with Bennett, and tried to reframe how she'd pictured him in her mind. She hadn't thought him a player, but she also realized she'd pictured him with at least a few steady girlfriends over the years. And was he not happy with his job? He gave her a concerned look and nodded his head toward Jules, as if asking if she needed to be saved. She shook her head slightly. He said something else to Bennett before he started walking in their direction.

The exchange did not go unnoticed by Jules. "But he's

drawn to you," Jules said, watching his brother come closer. "I just haven't seen that before."

Lia's heart skipped. She didn't know how to take that. She'd thought Jules was warning her away from Haydn, but it sounded like he was doing the opposite ... encouraging her to pursue him. "I'm not looking for a relationship," she said quietly, quickly, but Jules was already walking away, and Haydn took his place only a second later.

"Is he giving you grief about staying?" Haydn asked, a protective note in his tone.

"No, not at all," Lia assured him. Jules had unsettled her, but not for any reason Haydn was worried about. She didn't even want to consider being in a relationship again so soon. Especially not with someone who, according to Jules, would never leave Alaska. And could she blame him? She breathed in the fresh, outdoorsy air until it filled her lungs. It was gorgeous here. And quiet. It gave her creativity space to stretch.

"Did you get any good pictures yet?" she asked, in an attempt to distract herself. As he showed her his photo reel, though, she couldn't keep her mind off of what Jules said. Yet in the end, it didn't matter if she was ready for a relationship or not. Or if Haydn would leave Alaska or not. Because he didn't know who she really was, and she wasn't ready to tell him.

14

HAYDN

The morning stretched into a beautiful afternoon out on the coral-covered beach. They'd eaten the sandwiches and chips Bennett had prepared for them, and now the clouds had parted and the sun had sprung out to give them the kind of gorgeous sunny afternoon you didn't take for granted in southeast Alaska. Haydn had taken so many pictures, his memory card was nearly full—he had several extra back at the cabin, so it wasn't a big deal—but he still captured a few final pictures of the island bathed in poppy-yellow sunlight.

Lia had found a large, flat rock to lie out on, and had fallen asleep. Man, she was gorgeous.

He was eager to get back to the cabin and edit a few photos to send to his editor at the magazine. The idea of doing a more personal write-up of the island kept niggling at him, giving him the same kind of excitement he'd gotten when he'd thought of working for *Nature Adventure Magazine*. It confirmed that he'd made the right choice by passing up their job offer, and he was ready to dig into this new feature.

"I'm going to head back to get dinner started," Bennett said. "Should we wake her up?"

All three brothers looked out to where she slept. She appeared more at peace than she had since they'd met her, and he knew they were all loath to wreck that.

"I've got to send some emails," Jules said, "if you guys want to head back."

Haydn tried not to bristle at how quickly Jules offered to stay. Logically, he knew that Jules really did need to send some emails—he seemed to have a never-ending email task list—but he didn't have to be quite so eager about it.

He wasn't proud of it, but when he'd seen her talking to Jules earlier, a flare of jealousy had lit up inside of him. If Jules liked Lia, then Haydn wanted to stand back and let him have a chance at getting to know her. But his feet hadn't agreed, apparently, because the next thing he knew, he'd been heading in their direction to break up whatever conversation they'd been having. Who was he? He didn't do things like that, but the impulse had been impossible to deny.

As if to prove to himself that he could control his impulses, he agreed. Yet he nearly ran back to the cabin in his eagerness to finish editing his photos and get back to the hill to send them.

"Slow down!" Bennett complained, but Haydn pretended not to hear him.

When he got back to the cabin, he used a cord to move his pictures over to his laptop, groaning when every picture seemed to take forever to download. Bennett shook his head and muttered something under his breath as he got dinner started, but it seemed like he was fighting a smile. Whatever. Haydn would never understand his brothers.

He scrolled through the pictures, pausing on the few he'd taken with Lia in the background. There was one of her holding a starfish, and another of her hopping from one rock to another, blue ocean above her ankles. He'd also captured one of her lying on the rock—and it made his breath catch in his lungs. This was it. The perfect photo. She was only the smallest portion of the photo, while the rest of it was hill and flowers and endless sky. If he could capture what southeast Alaska felt like in one single image, it would be this.

He didn't take long to edit the photo—these wouldn't be going in the final article, but were merely to capture his editor's interest—and then moved them back over to his phone and raced out the door.

"Tell everyone dinner will be ready in an hour!" Bennett yelled after him, elbow deep in some sort of dough.

When Haydn got to the beach, he was sweaty and out of breath, but he didn't care. He scanned the beach, half expecting to find Jules and Lia snuggled together on the rock. His stomach twisted at the thought, and relief filled him when he realized the rock was empty.

He scanned farther down the beach, relieved to find Lia sitting on their picnic blanket, reading the book Bennett had finished earlier, and Jules was still up at the hill, emailing. Haydn resisted the urge to go straight to Lia and instead joined Jules. He'd been the one to discover that he could get one bar of signal at that location, and Haydn didn't want to know how many places he'd had to test out before he found it.

"Here to give me a hard time?" Jules asked distractedly, his fingers flying over his phone.

"No. I'm here to join you."

Jules looked up with a raised eyebrow as Haydn pulled out his phone and opened his email app. "You never email out here."

"I have a story idea I want to float past my editor at *Ridges*."

Jules grunted, and Haydn could tell his mind was already back on his work.

He wrote up a few sentences outlining what the photographs would be like, attached a zip file with several photos to showcase the location and style, and pressed send. Nerves swirled through him in a way they normally didn't anymore after he emailed his editor. He'd never proposed anything so personal before, either.

Lia's voice carried out to him on the wind, and he realized she was singing something. Like a sailor drawn in by a siren, he moved in her direction almost against his will. She smiled when she saw him, and any trepidation he might have been feeling fled. He picked up his pace.

"What are you singing?" he asked her.

"Just another made-up song," she told him. "I can't get over how incredible it is out here." She tipped her head toward the sky, and the sun kissed her smooth skin. "Do you get used to it?"

"I haven't yet. I hope I never do."

They walked side by side along the beach, their hands brushing occasionally but neither of them moving away to prevent it. He needed to stop this. She lived in Nashville. She'd just gone through a huge breakup. And this wasn't him—the longing and the jealousy and the stomach swirling and the intense desire to take her hand firmly in his—and see how her mouth tasted next.

Being near her had put him in some sort of haze, and he struggled to blink through it. Well, struggled to *want* to blink through it, and not just sink into it like he might a thick fog.

"I can't figure it out," she said. Her hand brushed his again, and he nearly groaned.

"What?"

"If it's this island that's magical ..." She paused—another hand brush—and her gaze met his. "Or if it's you."

He swallowed hard.

"You three, I mean," she added hurriedly. "You too, but— Forget I said anything."

He laughed. "I can't forget it. I'm magic; no take backs."

She nudged him with her shoulder. "You know what I meant."

He decided to stop teasing her. Hadn't he just been thinking how incredible this island was? Magic was the exact right word to describe it. "Yeah, I do."

"Whatever it is, I never want it to stop," she murmured so quietly, he wondered if he was supposed to hear it. Their hands collided again, and this time he gave in to the urge to slide his fingers between hers. He was gratified when her fingers clasped his back.

"Me neither," he said, just as quietly.

15

HAYDN

*H*aydn whistled as he got dressed in the bathroom, realizing how light and happy he felt. He never felt this happy in the morning, especially not before breakfast.

But all the loneliness he'd been grappling with for the last several months had fled, and in its place was a sense of belonging. Being on the island with his brothers was restorative. And being with Lia? Confusing, unnecessarily distracting, a bad idea. But also intoxicating, exhilarating, heady. And the side of him that craved sunlight over stormy days was winning.

He walked out of the bathroom with an extra skip to his step and was met with a face-full of pillow. The pillow fell to his feet, revealing a bed-headed, scowling Jules in the dim hall light. "No. Whistling." He went back to his bedroom and slammed his door shut.

"Seconded!" Bennett called from behind his closed door as if they were around a board table considering a proposal on the agenda.

They'd stayed up until past one in the morning, snacking and laughing and talking, and their plan had been to sleep late. But Haydn's ability to sleep in was suffering thanks to sleeping on a couch. And when he'd awoken, his first thought had been of Lia's smooth palm pressed into his.

Forget going back to sleep. Forget hating mornings. A day he got to wake up and see Lia was good day.

The door to Haydn's room—Lia's room?—was open, and she sat cross-legged on the bed, writing in a notebook. She wore a pair of rumpled red-and-black plaid pajama shorts and a black tank top. His heart skittered right over its next beat, seeing her look so comfortable in his bed. She didn't have makeup on, and she'd braided her hair into two loose braids that were slung over her slender, tan shoulders.

"Did my whistling wake you too?"

She glanced up at him, and then closed her notebook and set it on the tousled blanket. "I'll wake up to Billy Joel any day." She patted the bed beside her and tucked her feet beneath her to give him more space to sit.

The room had never seemed as small as it did when he sat on his bed next to Lia. He'd also never been so grateful that he'd opted for the twin size. Especially as Lia's folded knees brushed against his arm, causing him to catch his breath. "I think he's worse than me before breakfast."

She snickered, and he joined in, but they both stopped abruptly when Jules banged on the wall in warning.

"You're not so bad," she whispered as she moved closer. "In fact, I like you before breakfast."

He swallowed hard, but tried to look unaffected. "Huh. I like you before breakfast too. And all times of the day, come to think of it."

"I'm pretty likable," she teased breathily.

He leaned toward her like a fish being drawn in on a reel, and she tilted her head.

Jules banged again, and Lia's eyes twinkled with amusement as Haydn huffed impatiently.

Haydn's nose brushed her ear as he whispered, "Want to go on an adventure?"

~

Haydn lowered the dinghy from Bennett's boat and maneuvered it away from the island quietly, waiting until they were a good distance away from the cabin to let the engine roar. Lia sat across from him, the brightly colored hat from Bennett cinched under her chin, her braids peeking out from the brim.

It was too difficult to talk over the engine, so he enjoyed the view—of both the ocean and Lia. He inhaled the salty scent of ocean and mist, and navigated them around a few other small islands, most of them uninhabited.

Lia pointed to houses set on platforms on the water, and he saw them through her eyes. There were some Alaskan quirks he was so used to that he sometimes forgot how unique it all was.

Finally, they got to his favorite cove in all of Alaska. He slowed the dinghy until it coasted over the gentle waves and then came to a full stop. The drone of the engine silenced, leaving only the sound of water lapping on the hull.

"I can't get over how gorgeous it is here," Lia whispered. Sun shone on the blue-gray mountains in the distance. On all sides of them, like the hedges of a royal maze, massive pine trees rose up into the cerulean sky. He framed it in his mind as if looking through his viewfinder, and then gave in to the urge to pull out his camera and snap a few photos. When he aimed the camera at Lia, he paused to see if she'd say anything about not taking her picture.

When she didn't, he caught her in profile as she stared out over the water.

"You were made for this," he told her as he took a few more.

She shifted, and he saw the first few hints of her feeling uncomfortable. He shifted to take more pictures of the island behind her rather than making her the focus, though she was still the focus of his attention.

"Have you lived here your whole life?" Lia asked. She tilted her head up toward where the sun poked out of the clouds. He'd lent her one of his waterproof jackets—hers was still damp from exploring the tide pools—and it completely engulfed her body.

"Born and raised," he said. "We spent our childhood in Ketchikan, and then moved out to Winterhaven after our mom died."

"Oh, I'm sorry," Lia said. "You're the oldest, right?"

"I am." His grip tightened on the camera, and he knew the photos he was taking during this conversation weren't going to be any good, but he also wasn't willing to put down the shield of his camera. Even though they had been told their mom would die, even though she'd talked to them all and written letters and made sure her finances were in order, and even though her illness was the catalyst for their dad leaving—he hadn't been prepared emotionally. "Rosie had just graduated high school, and she needed a change. We all needed a change. Bennett had the opportunity to buy out an expedition business, so he decided to take it, and we all moved out to Winterhaven. Except for Jules, who was in Juneau at the University of Alaska Southeast at the time."

"Did you always know you wanted to be a photographer?" she asked.

Since this was a more comfortable topic, he finally put his camera down before he used up his entire memory card on unusable pictures of the ocean. "No. I wanted to be a doctor."

She nodded. "I can see it. So, what happened?"

"I studied biology for my undergrad and was applying to med schools when my mom died, and I knew I needed to stay home. I've been taking photos for several small-business websites in Alaska since I was in high school, and the editor at *Alaska Ridges* saw some of my photos and reached out to me to do some contract work. When they had an opening for a staff photographer, they asked me if I wanted to work with them full time. That was about five years ago, and I've been with them ever since."

"Do you think you'll ever go back to med school?" Lia asked. She pulled her legs up and wrapped her arms around her calves, resting her chin on her knees. The waves pushed at the boat, lulling him into a sense of peace, even though this part of his history was always intertwined with the biggest losses of his life—his plans of becoming a doctor, his dad, and then his mom.

"No. I can't imagine being in school again for so many years. And after the freedom of being a photographer and traveling through Alaska—it's hard to contemplate a job that would keep me indoors all day." On really cold nights, when he was camping and the light wasn't good enough for any pictures, or his feature articles were rejected over and over again—sometimes then he wondered what life would have been like if he'd been able to go to med school. But what-could-have-beens were a quick way to feeling miserable about life, and he wouldn't trade moving to Winterhaven with Rosie and Bennett for anything.

"Jules mentioned that your dad left too. That must have left you with a lot of responsibility."

Jules had told her about Dad? He hated talking about it. "It did, but I'm not resentful about it."

"I didn't mean to imply that you were. I can tell you're a great brother. They're lucky to have you."

The warmth from the sun shining down on him seeped all the way to his bones. "Thank you. Rosie might say otherwise.

She's constantly reminding us we're her brothers and not her dad." He smiled sardonically.

She stared at him in an appraising way that made him feel like his stomach was pitching and rolling, just like the dinghy. "It's good Rosie has you three."

"Who do you have?" he asked. It hadn't escaped his notice that when she was in crisis, her answer had been to come to the middle of nowhere, all alone. Did she have the equivalent of Rosie and his brothers in her life?

She ran her fingers along the rim of the dinghy and looked out on the horizon. "I don't trust a lot of people."

"Why not?"

"I've been used too many times. People think I can help them get ahead. Or forget I'm a person with feelings."

He felt his brows furrow with confusion. He was realizing how little he knew about her. She was great at asking questions and getting him and his brothers to open up, but she clammed up whenever they asked her about her life. He'd assumed it was because of the painful breakup she was still reeling from, but maybe there was more. "Is this through your job? Or do you just have really crappy people in your life?"

"Both?" She let out a short laugh.

"I'm realizing I don't know what you do."

She didn't say anything, and the silence turned awkward. He realized that she might not answer—that she might not want to let him in as easily as he'd just let her in. And who could blame her, if she'd had people treat her so poorly?

"I don't want to lie to you," she finally said. "But I also don't want to tell you what I do."

He frowned. Rosie thought she was running from something—was it the law? He couldn't see Lia doing anything illegal, but he also would protect his family first and always. "Is it legal?"

"Yes. And I'm making it sound really dramatic." She let out

a huff, but it seemed like it was directed toward herself and not at him. "People treat me different when they realize what I do."

"I won't."

"You will," she promised him, sounding sad.

Disappointment flooded him, and he realized how much he wanted her to trust him. To let him in. But he also knew, from Rosie, that banging around someone's emotional issues like an elephant in a sandcastle competition wasn't going to convince her of anything. Only his actions would—showing her he could be trusted. That they all could.

So he shifted away from asking her what she did, and went back to his original question, knowing his concern was as apparent as the red slash of paint on the dinghy's hull. "Who do you have in your life, Lia?"

Her shoulders eased with relief, and she released a self-deprecating laugh. "My assistant is pretty cool."

"What about someone not on your payroll?" he asked hesitantly.

"I had my ex and my best friend, before ..." She shrugged. "I have to be careful, even with family. I've had to set boundaries with my mom, who tends to speak before she thinks, and will say things at my expense if it gets her attention. And my dad is remarried with a twelve-year-old daughter and a nine-year-old son. They're cool, and I love them to pieces, but my dad's busy."

"Too busy for you?"

"I don't know. I'm afraid to test it."

He struggled to imagine what it would be like to not have anyone you knew with full certainty was in your corner. He trusted his brothers implicitly, and Rosie might drive them all nuts with her romcoms, money-making schemes, and general bossiness, but if any one of them showed up at her boat with a body, she'd grab a shovel, no questions asked.

"I know you don't know me well yet, but you can trust me.

And Jules and Bennett. And even Rosie—despite what this housing situation might lead you to believe about her."

Lia smiled softly. "I like her spirit. And how you all love her so fully."

"Do you want to hear my favorite Rosie story?"

She nodded, and he wondered if she was wanting to lighten the mood as much as him.

"When she was in seventh grade and I was in college, she went to each of my friends secretly and separately, and convinced them she needed help on her homework for a different class. For an entire semester, before I caught on, she had my friends doing all of her homework—one writing her English essays, one doing her math, and on and on. She wasn't happy when I put a stop to it."

"How did she convince them to do all that for her?"

He shook his head. "Rosie is our family's evil genius. She has a kind heart, so her intentions are usually good, but her results are a mixed bag."

"She's lucky to have the three of you."

"Lucky. Cursed." He put his hands to the side as if balancing a scale.

Lia reached forward, brought the hand he'd held up when he'd said "lucky," and pushed it up higher. His skin sizzled at her touch. They stared at each other for a long, heated moment.

"Lia," he whispered, his voice hoarse, but he didn't know how to finish that thought.

And luckily, he didn't have to. Because Lia brought her lips to his in a kiss that nearly knocked him off the boat. The dinghy rocked from side to side, and he gripped the edges to keep from toppling over. But he'd fall into the icy cold ocean before he'd pull away from Lia. This was why he always insisted on all dinghy passengers wearing a life vest.

Well, he'd never been in this *exact* situation for needing a life vest before, but he couldn't regret that he was now.

The boat rocked again, and Lia lost her balance and fell into him, breaking the contact from their kiss. "Oof," she said, her face making contact with his chest, right before her elbow drove into his lap.

He groaned and bent over on instinct, folding her into him.

"I'm so sorry!" she said.

"It's good," he wheezed out. "I need a second. Then we can pick up where we left off."

She covered her mouth with a small gasp.

"Are you laughing?" he wheezed out.

"No," she said through her fingers. "I feel really terrible, and would never laugh at ruining the moment in such a way."

He snorted, and then they were both laughing, though his was interspersed with groaning. "For the record, laughing does not help."

"Sorry," she said, wiping tears of mirth from her eyes as she continued to giggle, sounding anything but sorry. "I've never done that before during a kiss. Like, how did it even happen?"

Haydn watched her, loving how unguarded and relaxed she looked as she broke into another round of giggles. It was conta-gious—and yes, it was ridiculous. "Well, if it's any consolation, that's never happened to me before while kissing."

"Good to know I'm an original," she said. "And I really am sorry. And mortified."

"You sure sound like it," he said dryly, doing his best Jules imitation, but then waved his hand in the air. "It's no big deal. I'm sure one of my brothers will father a child for me on my behalf."

"Oh, geez. They probably would. I vote Bennett. He's the nicest one."

"Yeah, but no one would dare cross Jules."

"True." Her giggles finally subsided. Sometime during her

laughter, while he'd been recovering, she'd moved to sit beside him on the bench. Her leg, hip, and arm were pressed against his, and she stared up at him in an admiring way that nearly dissolved any self-discipline he had, making him want to pull her into his arms and endanger whatever appendage might be risked by another boat-kiss with her.

"You laugh more than anyone I've ever met," she said to him, like she was just figuring something out.

"Is that a good thing or a bad thing?"

"The best thing," she told him.

Warmth filled him as she linked her arm in his and rested her head against his bicep. He stared down at her lime-clad head, wondering if she could feel the way his heart raced, inches from where her cheek pressed against him.

"Look," she whispered.

He followed where she pointed to see a pod of sea otters swimming together, their little heads poking up from the water to check them out. "I see four of them," he whispered. His words stirred up the little hairs near her ear, and she shivered.

"Me too," she breathed without moving.

One otter broke away and swam a little closer, checking them out.

"Hi, buddy," Haydn said softly.

It cocked its head, then dove under the water and resurfaced back with its pod as if reporting his observations.

Lia sighed against him, and he wrapped his arm around her and tugged her into his side. What was he going to do? Everything about Lia screamed Bad Idea: he didn't know her job, she had trust issues, she lived in Tennessee and he lived in Alaska ... always and forever.

Most importantly, he didn't want a relationship that would shake up his life and change everything.

Except he very much did ... with Lia Hall. He wanted to show her he could be trusted. He wanted to bring her into the

Forrester group, the same way the otters welcomed each other back into their pods. He wanted to show her what it was like to have people who would always have your back no matter what.

He wanted to feel her lips against his again, and never, ever let go. And that scared him.

So, for now, he would just focus on being in the moment. A summer fling, apart from the real world. A happy for now, instead of a happily ever after. Rosie hated happy-for-now storylines, where the characters wouldn't end up together forever. But he understood the appeal. And if that's all he could have with Lia—and it was—it would have to be enough.

16

LIA

*L*ia sat alone on the porch and strummed a new song on her guitar as the sun lowered in the sky. She looked out over the water that gently lapped against the shore and let her fingers go where they wanted on the strings.

Meanwhile, her mind also went where it wanted to go—and in this case, it wanted to go straight to kissing Haydn Forrester.

What would it take for that to happen again? Whatever it was, she'd do it. Knowing Haydn, it wouldn't be much. Probably a smile from her, a lean in his direction, and he'd lean right back toward her.

Instead of give and take with Haydn, it felt like give and give. Both of them reaching for the other at the same time without any expectation for what was in it for them.

Could being with someone be so simple? No drama. No using or abusing or lying or cheating. Just bubbles of happiness floating through every sense.

He doesn't know who you are, Inner Gwen reminded, her taunting tone like a sharp needle poking all those bubbles. When Haydn had asked her straight-out, she'd debated lying.

Pretending she could really be Lia Hall, a teacher—or a rideshare driver or a sound engineer—from Tennessee. But she'd had too many people lie to her to ever want to lie to someone she cared about.

And she cared about Haydn. A lot. A growing lot.

She wished she had someone she could talk to about this. *Who do you have?* Haydn's question ran through her mind once again, as it had since he'd asked. On the surface, she had countless people who adored her: her fans, who were pretty incredible, and her staff, who made sure she put out a good product. But none of them really knew her on a deep level. They didn't know that she longed to have a close relationship with her half-siblings, but also worried about accidentally dragging them into the limelight. They didn't know that she'd been thinking of ending things with Bo for almost six months before he'd broken up with her. Had she noticed he was distant, and that was why she'd wanted to break things off? She hadn't even told Gwen any of that.

Gwen. The one person she would have sworn she could trust, and who now liberally shared private details about her life to the media. It wasn't like she had any deep and dark secrets, but in a life so public, it had been nice to have some things that were just her own.

And the only way to ensure things stayed that way was to remain alone. It had seemed like the only sensible solution before she'd met Haydn, but now ...

Her fingers had mindlessly started to play a song about five-hundred miles. Then another about a thousand years. She rested her fingers on the strings and closed her eyes.

Okay, subconscious, I get it. Long-distance relationships are a thing. That doesn't solve my trust issues.

She set her guitar back in the case before her subconscious delivered her songs about trust. It was too soon to be thinking any of this anyway. They'd just met. And he didn't know the most important thing about her. She hadn't lied outright, but wasn't a lie of omission the same thing? He lived a quiet life, and her life was anything but quiet.

The men were out on the beach, throwing a Frisbee back and forth. Haydn's now-familiar laugh sounded deeply through the trees, and she realized she didn't care that it hadn't been very long since they'd met, and even if it made no sense at all … she'd completely fallen for him.

She sang songs about this kind of thing happening—love at first sight. Relationships being meant to be. Feelings and emotions that were bigger than words.

Did she really believe any of that was real? Even after everything that had happened to her?

Yes, she did. Despite everything, she really did.

~

Haydn's brothers were a lot of things, but subtle was not one of them. They must have noticed a different vibe between Lia and Haydn after their kiss in the dinghy—or perhaps one of them caught the two holding hands under the table during breakfast—but suddenly they were too busy to go out and explore.

And they were full of ideas for romantic-sounding excursions.

A picnic in the trees.

Kayaking through the bay.

Tonight? Stargazing at midnight on the beach.

Haydn brought his camera, as always, though he'd set it beside him on the blanket. They lay side by side, staring up into the endless sea of stars above them.

"Sometimes the fog is too thick to see the stars, but Bennett and Jules must have pulled some strings to get a clear night."

He turned his head to look at her, and she looked at him, and they both laughed.

"Do they think they're being sneaky?" she asked.

"Probably, but they lack the finesse Rosie would have added to their matchmaking schemes."

"It seems like it's working out pretty well to me," she said, squeezing his hand. "Have you checked yet to see if your editor wants your story?"

"No. I think I'll wait until I get home." He let out a sigh that was heavier than she expected. "I'm not quite sure what I'll do if they turn it down. Just the same thing I've been doing, I guess." He tried to laugh it off, but it sounded like a nervous laugh.

She lifted herself up on her elbow so she could look down into his face. "There are other magazines."

He wouldn't meet her eyes. "Yeah. But none with national reach like *Ridges* does."

"I mean outside of Alaska."

He didn't say anything and still wouldn't look at her.

"It's going to be a good story, Haydn. I don't want to see it disappear." All week, while they'd been going on their adventures—or not-so-subtly set-up dates—he'd told her all about the feature he wanted to write. The excitement lit up his eyes whenever he talked about how he wanted to frame it, or what stories he'd share, or what photographs he'd pair with it. He went into details about color and texture and the importance of variety.

She couldn't imagine anyone ever not being interested in Haydn's stories. While he photographed and wrote down notes about the stories he could tell, she wrote song lyrics that flowed from her as fluidly as the shoulder-high waterfall Haydn had taken her to yesterday. Apparently, he and his brothers would sometimes skinny-dip in the ice-cold, shoulder-deep water. And they would race down the beach—the loser having to do all their laundry for the week. And they'd spend hours scouring for seashells for their mom's collection, which Rosie now kept on her boat. All stories he wanted to include in his feature somehow.

The story of this island was really the story of the Forrester brothers. And Lia couldn't get enough—especially of Haydn. She wanted her hand in his. Her cheek on his shoulder. Her arms around his waist. Her mouth pressed against his. She wanted to breathe in the fresh, outdoorsy scent of him and taste the sea salt on his lips, touch the warmth of his skin, immerse her every sense in him.

She suspected he felt the same. His arm wrapped easily around her shoulders whenever she sat beside him on the couch. He found excuses to tickle her side and make her giggle, or to brush imaginary hairs away from her face. He watched her in a way that made her forget that it wasn't just the two of them alone in a room, but that Jules and Bennett were there too. Until they weren't, and she'd blink her eyes to find that the two other Forrester brothers had slipped from the room while Lia was caught in Haydn's spell.

It was hard to believe that an entire week had nearly passed. It was almost time for Lia to go home. Time to face reality. She didn't want to. Wasn't ready for it yet. Didn't want to think about it.

So she wouldn't.

Instead, she snagged Haydn by the front of the sweater and pulled him close for a kiss that made her every sense curl up like a kitten before a golden fire.

17

HAYDN

The cabin had never felt so like home than it did right then. Bennett was reading a book on birds indigenous to Alaska—with a highlighter in hand. Jules played solitaire with an actual deck of cards. Lia strummed her guitar, stopping occasionally to jot something down in the notebook beside her, before continuing again.

And Haydn sat on the couch, attempting to read a thriller, but he'd barely made it a hundred pages in and realized he couldn't even say what the last chapter he'd read was about.

Instead, his mind and gaze kept wandering to Lia and her magical, effortless connection with the music she was creating. She fit so seamlessly into the dynamic with his brothers—where they could all be in the same room, doing separate activities, but in the same space. Where Bennett might read aloud some interesting fact he'd learned about puffins. Or Jules would make his self-satisfied grunt-laugh when he won another round. Or his frustrated grunt-snarl when he was stuck, and Haydn leaned forward and moved the right card for him like it was easy.

He never dreamed he'd meet a woman who not only understood the dynamic of him and his brothers, but could so easily slip into it.

"I like that," Bennett said to her when she hit on a particular chord progression.

"Hmm. What about this?" she asked, changing something Haydn couldn't explain but somehow made the sound even fuller. He knew Lia didn't need Bennett's input or approval—or any of theirs—but she seemed to like these small interactions within their separate activities.

"That's the one."

She smiled softly in response. RIP, Haydn's reading comprehension. He might as well have been reading one of Jules's legal briefs for all he was retaining.

He recalled learning about parallel play in school—where children often played different things in the same room together. He and his brothers had never grown out of that. He didn't know if it was having their father leave and their mother die soon after that bonded them, or being close in age. Sometimes they'd joke that they were meant to come as triplets, but Haydn was too eager to be born to wait for Bennett, who had probably gotten derailed watching some sort of animal, while Jules had been distracted by something Rosie was doing.

Lia jotted down something else, then set her guitar in the case before heading toward the bathroom. The door had barely clicked closed behind her before Haydn felt two sets of eyes burning into his.

"What are you going to do?" Bennett asked. He'd set his book face-down on the coffee table and pulled his socked feet under him on his favorite chair.

Haydn tried to pull his mind away from the haze that listening to Lia—just being with her—put him in. "About what?"

Jules let out a disgusted huff.

"Lia," Bennett said slowly. "She goes home tomorrow."

Haydn had been doing his very best not to think about that. Instead, he'd rather think about Lia's mouth pressed against his, and how silky her long, blond hair felt when he ran his fingers through it.

Even more, he loved the tender lilt to her voice when she talked about music. Or the way her laughter made him feel like he was surfing above the foamy waves. He knew trust didn't come easily to her, but he'd seen her slowly opening up to him over the last few days of adventuring together on the island.

"You've lost him again." Jules lightly knocked Haydn on the side of the head. "Earth to Haydn."

Haydn blinked and tried to get his head back into the present. The problem was, he didn't want to. Because after tomorrow, he and Lia wouldn't see one another again. She'd fly back to Nashville and her private life there, and he'd head to Winterhaven—and either work on his feature article or go back to taking photos for the magazine of the same places he'd been to dozens of times before.

Eventually, probably sooner than he hoped, he'd be a mere speck in her memory. An interesting side note of a time spent in Alaska.

While he knew he'd never forget her.

Bennett nudged him, a little harder than Jules had.

"What's to figure out?" Haydn said, annoyed. "This was one of those summer romances, and when she leaves, it's done."

"Nope." Bennett shook his head firmly. "What you two have is real."

"I agree," Jules said. "Which means the vote is two against one."

"My love life does not come with voting rights."

"Oh, but it does," Jules said. "Because we have to deal with whoever you end up with, and we like her."

"A lot," Bennett added.

They were giving Haydn a headache. He lowered his forehead to his hands.

"Do I have voting rights?"

At the sound of Lia's voice, Haydn reared his head back so quickly, he cracked his head against Bennett's, and both of them fell back against the couch.

"I'm bleeding," Bennett said. "Dang it. You hit my nose."

"Is it broken?" Haydn asked. His head throbbed, and he blinked to clear his vision.

"I don't know."

"Let me see." Jules had broken his nose at least twice while playing basketball in high school. He was a magnet for stray elbows. He studied Bennett's nose, and a moment later, Lia handed him a damp towel to give to Bennett.

Bennett took the towel gratefully. "I knew you were hard-headed, but ..." He attempted to joke as he dabbed at the blood.

"Doesn't look broken," Jules declared. "But it does need some ice, and it's going to leave you with one heck of a headache." He paused in front of Haydn and said in a low voice, "I've got this. You two should talk."

Lia stood in the doorway with a closed-off expression, one he hadn't seen since her first day at the cabin. He imagined Rosie slapping the back of his head. *She was just starting to trust you, and you've gone and blown it.*

But weren't they on the same page when it came to being together? They had some insurmountable things that would keep them apart—and he'd assumed she was just in it for the week too. It wasn't that he didn't want to keep seeing her. He couldn't even think about the moment she'd leave the island without feeling like he was climbing Denali behind an intense guide determined to race daylight.

He didn't want to have this conversation. But even more, he couldn't bear to think that he might have hurt her. He winced as he recalled what she might have overheard. "Are you up for a hike?" She didn't respond right away, and before she could formulate an excuse, he said, "I want to show you something."

She lifted a brow. "Do I get a vote in *that*?"

He cringed. "If you'd rather not—"

"Of course I want to come." She shook her head and went into her bedroom without another word.

"Dude," Bennett said in a nasal voice, shaking his head. "Sometimes you make life hard on purpose."

"No, I don't."

"Uh, yeah. You do." Jules started counting off on his fingers. "Staying at a job you don't love because you're afraid to leave us. Helping Rosie with her last *three* doomed-to-fail fundraising schemes. Resisting being in a relationship with the perfect girl for you."

Jules ... wasn't wrong.

"Wait, I don't hate my job."

"Please," Bennett said with an eye roll. "We're not as clueless as you seem to think we are."

He tried to settle his thoughts on one point—they knew?—so he could argue with them. But all potential arguments with his brothers fled from his mind as Lia walked out of her room wearing his waterproof jacket zipped over her T-shirt and shorts. Her hair was in two braids again, her signature island look. More than anything, he wanted to stride across the room, pull her into his arms, and beg her to stay with him.

Beg her to trust him. To let him into her life and see all the parts of her she was hiding from him. To be smarter than him and push him away, because he didn't know if he'd have the stamina to do it if she wasn't pushing too.

"Ready?" he said gruffly instead.

Bennett narrowed his eyes, while Jules gave him an *Are you serious right now?* look.

"Ready," Lia said lightly, and she took his arm like they were going to a ball.

18

LIA

When she leaves, it's done.

Lia followed Haydn outside, feeling the gazes of Bennett and Jules on her back before the door closed between them. The rain came down in a steady drizzle, so she zipped up her jacket and flipped the hood over her hair. It served to both keep her head dry and help her avoid having to look at Haydn.

Inside the hoodie, it was easy to pretend she was alone again. On this island, all by herself, like she'd originally planned. It wasn't the comforting thought she'd hoped it would be. She'd never been so grateful to have her original plans thwarted.

This week was a two-edged sword. Now she knew what she'd been missing. She hadn't known relationships could be like this. It could be light and fun and easy, but also deep and meaningful. It could make her feel safe, both inside and out. You couldn't miss something you'd never experienced, and now that she had, she'd spend the rest of her life longing for it again. Because she'd never settle for anything less.

That's what she'd done with Bo—settle. She'd mistaken

their creative energy for love. Whenever he'd put himself first, she'd told herself that it was healthy for partners to be apart—and the fact that she was relieved to have a break from him was a normal aspect of adult relationships. When he'd ignored her for weeks on end, she'd convinced herself he was protecting his creative flow.

When he'd taken portions of her lyrics without permission and given them to other artists, she'd told herself it was a compliment. Or that he was forgetful. Or that he was a horrible person, but weren't they all horrible at one time or another? And it wasn't unforgivable.

She'd been upset at all the lies Bo and Gwen told her, but she was realizing the person who had lied to her the most was herself. She hadn't wanted to face the truth, and so she'd created a relationship she was comfortable with—one that never let her be completely vulnerable.

And she still hesitated to be vulnerable. She'd kept her guard up with Bo—and look what happened there. She'd lost the twelve amazing songs they'd co-written, and her best friend, and maybe even her reputation. She glanced sideways at Haydn. Being with him thrilled her as much as singing a new song, in that moment when everything came together and blended just right. She'd let her guard down with him, bit by bit and day by day, but even still he didn't know everything.

And even still, the words caught on her tongue before she could speak them out loud.

I'm Aurelia Halifax. I'm still the girl who loves grilled cheese and napping in the sunlight and singing notes and lyrics that don't always sound good or make sense together.

I'm still me, just famous.

What if he'd heard the lies Bo and Gwen had spread about her? What if he believed them?

The thought made her voice catch in her throat, made it impossible to speak. She couldn't take the chance. She'd felt so hurt when she'd overheard him calling what they had a summer romance, but maybe he was right. No, he *was* right. She just hadn't wanted to face it.

On this island, it felt like anything was possible. But outside of it, nothing was. She'd take the boat back to the island and the plane back to Nashville, and she'd be stuffed so tightly into the Aurelia Halifax box, she wouldn't be able to breathe or think or see or stretch out, much less have enough space for a whole other person.

It was decided, then. So where was the relief?

As they drew closer to the western shore of the island, she heard the crackling of seaweed and coral that indicated low tide. Tall pine trees towered on all sides of them until they broke free of the tree line to an open beach that slid into a receded ocean.

Where the north side of the island had been rocky, this side contained a beach with an enormous hill of sparkling white. She caught her breath at the sight of it—almost like diamonds on the beach, with the way the light hit them. "What in the world ...?"

"Shells."

She bent over and picked up a handful of the little white shards, some sharp and some smooth. They were bigger than grains of sand, but smaller than pebbles. "It's so pretty."

"There's a group of seals who like the island's buffet, and they leave behind these shells." He peered out toward the horizon. "Look."

She followed his finger to see a tiny head bobbing up in the water, maybe forty feet from shore. Lia's breath caught, and she was suddenly feeling emotional. It was easier to think it was because of the novelty of seeing a seal than because of Haydn—and wasn't she a pro at lying to herself? "There have to be millions of shells here."

"Yep."

"It reminds me of a poem in *Through the Looking Glass*. 'The Walrus and the Carpenter.'"

Haydn laughed, but it sounded almost forced. "I haven't thought of that in ages." He walked out to a wide pile of shells and sat. Their little seal friend popped his head up closer and then farther back again, as if he was just as curious about them as they were about him.

Lia sat beside Haydn, close enough to touch if she wanted to, but she kept her hands to herself. They both watched the seal bob around the small peninsula. After a moment, another head bobbed up to join the first. Lia hugged her legs to her chest and rested her chin on her knees.

"My mom got sick when I was twelve." Haydn let a handful of shells stream between his fingers to a small pile near his legs. "For over a year, she did tests and visited specialists to try to figure out what was wrong, but they couldn't. Eventually, she couldn't get out of bed. And ten years later, she died."

Lia held her breath, afraid that if she made even the smallest of sounds, he might stop talking.

"My dad left us a month after my sixteenth birthday."

Lia swiveled to look at him, but he kept his gaze on the seal as though it might hold the secrets of the universe. The only sign that he might still have some feelings about what he said was the tightening of his jaw as he continued.

"Bennett was fourteen, Jules thirteen. Rosie was only eight. He used to send cards occasionally. Or a phone call here or there. Those eventually dropped off, and none of us have spoken to him in five years."

Five years. That's when their mom had died. Oh, Haydn. It put her own problems into perspective. To lose both parents like that had to be like having the ground beneath your feet open up into an unexpected chasm. And he'd been bridging it for his siblings ever since.

"And part of me wonders if I'm not destined to be like my

dad. Leave the people I love." His voice drifted off quieter, almost like he was talking to himself.

"You would never do that," she said, with more vehemence than she'd intended.

He turned to her with a sardonic twist of his mouth. "I'm in a different city every week, taking photographs for the magazine. Half the time, they don't know where I am. And the worst part—I love traveling and exploring new places. I'd love to get out of Alaska and explore the world, but I won't let myself. I can't."

Lia gave up trying to keep the wall between them, and she scooted close enough to grab his hand and hold it with both of hers. "That doesn't mean you'll abandon them."

"I don't trust myself."

"Well, I trust you." Her words hovered between them, and she realized the truth of them. So she could still recognize truth when she saw it.

And she could still trust. She tightened her grip on his hand, feeling lighter than before, even in this heavy moment. What if she could finally just stop lying? To herself. To Haydn.

"I'm Aurelia Halifax." She blurted it out so quickly, she wasn't sure if Haydn understood her. She hoped he had, because her heart was racing faster than right before she got on stage. It was a blend of both excitement and terror, and it would fuel her with energy for several hours.

Out here, on this quiet patch of seashells, that energy really didn't have anywhere to go. Except into squeezing Haydn's hand.

"What?" His brows drew low over his eyes.

She took a deep, steadying breath and forced herself to speak slower. "My name isn't Lia Hall. It's Aurelia Halifax."

"Okay ..."

Ugh. He still wasn't getting it. She was going to have to spell it out.

See? Not everyone knows who you are, Inner Gwen said gleefully.

Shut it, Lia retorted, stuffing the sound of that critical voice as far back into her brain as she could. Inner Gwen had absolutely zero place in this moment.

She didn't know how else to get him to understand who she was, other than to sing. So she started with the first line of her most famous song, "Unsteady in Love." She'd been careful not to sing any of her own songs this week when she'd been messing around on her guitar, instead sticking to classic songs that everyone knew all the words to.

Haydn continued to look at her in confusion, and then there was the beat—the very moment—she saw it click for him. His eyes widened, and to her disappointment, he pulled his hand away from hers and scrambled a few feet away from her, knocking over his pile of shells.

She stopped singing and just watched him, waiting for him to say something. Myriad emotions ran across his face, and she wished she knew him well enough to read them all. She wanted to believe that was understanding in his expression, and not anger. Or maybe it was disgust and regret.

She tugged at her braid, unable to keep her hands steady as she watched and waited.

"Why didn't you tell me?" he asked, his voice hoarse.

"Everyone treats me different once they know who I am. I just wasn't ready for that. I wanted to be Lia Hall for the week."

His eyes clouded. That was definitely anger. He stood and marched a few more steps away before turning back to face her. "Was any of it real, then? I was falling in love with Lia Hall, and she doesn't exist."

Falling in love? Her heart raced, and it took effort for her to focus on what Haydn was saying. On not regretting telling him sooner, while knowing that she never could have told him before now. Not until she knew she trusted him. "It was *all* real."

"Then tell me something real! I don't know what to believe."

She stood and stepped toward him, but stayed far enough away to give him the space he seemed to need. "Six weeks ago, I discovered my boyfriend, Bo, and my best friend, Gwen, had been in a secret relationship together for almost three months."

That was something the tabloids didn't know. Bo and Gwen said they'd fought their feelings for months, and the day she'd discovered them kissing was the day they'd finally given in to the urge to be together.

"Neither of them wanted to end their relationship with me while I was finishing writing songs for my latest album. An album they stole from me, and Gwen just released this week."

Another thing the tabloids didn't know. They'd replaced Gwen's name with hers, erased her as if she didn't exist, when those songs were so deeply her own. But even if she got them back, they were tainted. She'd never be able to sing them.

"Then they started rumors to destabilize me and make it harder for people to believe me if I did accuse them of stealing. They made it sound like I was violent and unhinged, that they'd both been abused by me over the years and had found comfort in one another."

That one *was* all over the tabloids. Someone had taken a picture of her in the moment after she'd learned Bo and Gwen had betrayed her. She'd been distraught, crying, her makeup smeared, and for once, she hadn't been thinking of her image.

And the photo, paired with every play on her number one song "Unsteady in Love" as headlines, was shared across the world. No truth required. Her side of the story, even if she was willing to share it, was unnecessary and muddying to the truly sensational headlines people craved.

"I came out here because I needed a place to hide. I wanted to sleep away the entire week and forget any of this existed."

She moved closer, just a tiny step, and he didn't back away. She tried not to let the hope rise too high in her. "And instead, I was surprised by you. You didn't know who I was, or what I'd been through, or all the lies they'd told about me, and I didn't want to give that up. You and your brothers treated me like a normal person, and it's been so long since I've experienced that. I'm sorry, Haydn."

Haydn closed his eyes and then pinched the bridge of his nose. "I don't know where to go from here, Lia. Aurelia. I don't even know what to call you."

"I prefer Lia with my friends."

He stared into her face as if taking her in, now knowing who she was. He shook his head. "I can't believe I didn't see it before now. Rosie loves your music. She even flew to Seattle to go to your last concert."

People usually only saw what they expected to see. And if he'd been expecting the Aurelia of the tabloids, maybe he would have seen that too. He still could. But she hoped he wouldn't.

He cleared his throat. "I'm sorry, Lia. This is going to take me a minute to process."

"That's okay. Take as long as you need." Disappointment swirled in her, though. She'd hoped that he would tell her that none of it mattered. That he'd sweep her into his arms and kiss her the same way he had last night, long and deeply and unforgettably. They still had one night left of their summer romance. She wasn't ready for it to end.

But the chasm between them seemed too large to cross.

He cleared his throat. "We should head back to the house."

"Oh." She nodded and fought back tears. "Yeah, sure."

About a foot separated them as they went back toward the house. "How's the legal battle going?"

"Legal battle?"

"For your songs. They stole your intellectual property."

"I haven't pursued legal action yet. I've been reeling, to be honest."

"Jules does IP work. We can ask him about it when we get back."

Her heart sank. She didn't want the rest of them to know yet, but she had to trust them too.

"It's not right they stole your songs."

"I don't want them back."

"Maybe not," he said fiercely. "But you should be getting royalties for them. If anything, it undercuts what they're making."

"You don't have to do this," she said to him.

"Do what?"

"Take care of me." She didn't want to be a burden to him. Someone who crashed into his life unexpectedly and then took from him.

"Lia ..." He paused as if gathering his thoughts. "Let me do this. Let us do this. It's what friends do."

"Friends?" A word had never cut so sharp while also sounding so exactly right. She didn't know what was up or down in this conversation.

"Yep." The main cabin came into view, and he pulled her to a stop. He hung his head down, and his cheeks were pink. "Look, Lia. I'm sorry if I made you uncomfortable this week, when I held your hand or"—he gulped—"kissed you."

"Haydn, no—"

He interrupted before she could finish. "I didn't know who you were, obviously, and I'm sure you get a lot of creeps coming on to you. I promise I won't be one of them."

"That's not what this was," she insisted. "I held your hand too."

"Right." He smiled wryly. "Anyway, friends?" He held out his hand for her to shake, and she wanted to push it away. She wanted to scream and cry and act like the person everyone thought she was when they saw the picture of her going crazy.

If she'd thought her heart had broken with Bo, she'd had no idea.

"Friends," she said, her voice cracking.

He looked at her carefully as he shook her hand like he might shake the hand of his editor over lunch, and then dropped it just as quickly. He walked ahead of her into the house with square shoulders and didn't look back.

She took an extra second to compose herself. Why had she told him who she was? Maybe they could have gone their entire lives without him realizing.

No, that was just wishful thinking. And it was better she told him. No more lies. Not to Haydn. Not to herself. And not to the world. It was time to tell everyone her side of the story.

But not yet. She still had one more night. She could be friends with Haydn. It was better than nothing. And she'd planned on letting things end tomorrow anyway. What was one day early?

Then why did it feel like she'd just lost the best thing of her entire life?

19

HAYDN

*H*aydn felt Lia's gaze on his shoulders as he set the table for dinner. His brothers kept shooting him questioning glances, and he knew they could tell that something had changed between him and Lia.

Aurelia.

Aurelia Halifax.

He was having a hard time wrapping his head around it. And how he hadn't seen it from the beginning. Now that he knew, it was all he could see. He must have looked ridiculous to her, making moves on her. A woman like Aurelia could have any man in the world.

He closed his eyes and let himself remember for just a moment what it was like to have her fingers curl around his, like she'd wanted to be there. Like they belonged with each other. Nope. That was not reality. They didn't belong with one another, and for more reasons than who she was.

They sat down to an awkward dinner. Lia sat beside Haydn, as usual, and he was torn between wishing she wasn't so painfully close, and being grateful he didn't have to stare at her all through dinner.

"Were the seals out today?" Bennett asked into the silence.

"They were," Lia said. She pushed her food around her plate but hadn't taken any bites yet. Haydn wasn't faring that well, either. Bennett had cooked his specialty—grilled salmon with a teriyaki glaze served over coconut rice. It was one of Haydn's favorite meals, yet tonight, it tasted like sand.

Once his brothers were done eating, Haydn popped up and took their plates, insisting he do the dishes for them. Lia didn't offer to help this time. She went into the living room and grabbed her guitar from the case.

He expected her to go outside to play, like she usually did, but this time, she sat on the couch. "Do you guys mind if I play in here tonight? It looks a little windy."

Haydn glanced out the window to where the trees blew wildly in the wind. He did mind hearing her play. How in the world was he supposed to keep his distance if she started to sing?

Just remember who she is and who you are, Haydn. That should do the trick.

Right. A backwoods Alaskan stuck in his ways and a massively talented worldwide superstar. He wanted to groan now, remembering some of their old conversations. How Bennett had bragged about him being a big deal because he had pictures in a local magazine. She'd been on the cover of countless magazines.

"What's going on?" Bennett said quietly as he came over to help clean. Jules sat beside Lia on the couch and said something that made Lia laugh. He tried not to writhe with jealousy. Sure, they were still getting along great. Jules didn't know who he was talking to.

"Nothing," Haydn said.

"Bull." Bennett stepped right in Haydn's way so he couldn't keep zooming back and forth around the kitchen to avoid making eye contact. "What happened out there?"

"It doesn't matter, Ben. She goes home tomorrow."

"Yeah, but I thought you guys—"

"Well, you thought wrong," he said, shutting the conversation down.

Bennett looked like he might say something more, but Haydn walked away before he could. He went into the bathroom to wash his hands and get some space. He knew he was being a jerk, but how could he explain something he didn't even understand himself?

Why did it bother him so much to learn she was Aurelia Halifax?

But he knew why—he just didn't want to admit it. A part of him had hoped that they might find a way to stay in touch once she left the island. That he wouldn't actually have to let her go. But their worlds were too different, and now he saw the week in an entirely different light. One where he was falling hard, while she was just having fun.

Not at his expense, though—he didn't believe Lia would ever treat someone that poorly or use him to distract herself. He'd become more invested in their relationship than she had. And it stung.

But it was for the best.

He pressed his palms to the counter and stared at himself. He needed to stick to the plan—write his feature for *Ridges* and focus on his family. One week with someone couldn't change years of focus.

Now if only he could believe it.

20

LIA

*L*ia played chord after chord, attempting to calm her thoughts. They buzzed around her mind like bees in a picnic, alighting on thoughts of Haydn, then starfish, then Alaska, then the Forrester brothers, and finally how much she wished things could be different.

That she really *was* Lia Hall.

That she didn't have to leave tomorrow.

That Haydn was still holding her hand and kissing her, instead of avoiding her eyes and hiding out in the bathroom.

"Play something we can sing to," Jules said. "I think we could use the distraction." He'd been great all night—buffering Haydn's offishness and making sure she still felt included. She wanted to talk to him about the IP suit, but not yet. She wasn't ready to be shut out by all of the Forrester brothers.

She slid into playing an old song her dad always loved. He'd taught her to play guitar when she was only nine years old, and the two of them would sing together often. Usually while her mom cleaning up after dinner or getting ready for bed. She hadn't thought about that in years.

Jules's low baritone voice started with the first line, and

Bennett drifted over from the kitchen next, singing along as well, without a hint of self-consciousness. To Lia's surprise, by the second verse, even Haydn had come out of the bathroom to sit on the ground by the fireplace—about as far away as he could get while still being in the room—and poke around with the knobs. But she heard his tenor voice join in with his brothers.

None of them were going to make it in Nashville anytime soon, but what they lacked in tone, they made up for in growing enthusiasm and lyrical knowledge. They knew every song she seamlessly transitioned into, from the Beatles to Top Forty hits.

When was the last time she'd sat around and played casually with a group? She hadn't sung yet—her throat still felt tight from holding back emotion, but with every song, it loosened more. This was her happy place. How had she forgotten?

A get-together with friends used to always include her pulling out her guitar for sing-alongs. It had a way of bringing the group together, lowering barriers, relaxing everyone.

At some point, singing had become both extremely private while also being massively public. Private and singular, in that she only ever felt connected with music deeply when she was alone. When she was with Bo, it had always felt like work, not play. Before then, music had been about connection. Her soul engaging with the souls of everyone close to her, in the notes and lyrics and rhythm of the song.

Without thinking, her fingers did the trapeze walk over the strings into one of her own songs, the placement and notes as familiar as her own face, and she began to sing. It was time to stop being afraid. To stop holding back. To connect and let people into her life and trust again.

Bennett gasped, and she continued playing as she looked up to find his eyes wide, his hands flailing in front of him like he was trying to stop a train with the force of his will. His mouth moved like he might say something, but only an airy squeak came out.

Jules sang along without missing a beat, surprising her by knowing every single word to the song. And it wasn't even one of her most popular hits, like "Unsteady in Love" was. It was one of the first songs she'd ever written, and it was still one of her favorites. Jules didn't seem to care that only the two of them sang, while Bennett was maybe losing more oxygen than safe.

Jules definitely had layers beneath that serious, button-up-shirt façade.

Lia's secret was officially not a secret anymore.

"Aurelia Halifax," Bennett finally breathed out as she finished the song and slid back into playing soft chord progressions. Bennett grabbed Jules by the arm he was leaning on, nearly toppling his brother. "One of the biggest voices in country music—ever."

Jules shook him off with an irritated huff. "Yeah. I know."

Bennett swiveled toward Haydn with an accusatory glare.

Haydn shrugged and said, "Yep."

Bennett looked at Lia next, his mouth still gaping before he put his hand to his head like he had a headache. "I'm processing. I don't understand what's happening right now. Aurelia Halifax in Alaska. In our cabin."

Lia stopped playing, and the silence seemed bigger than the music and their singing had been. "I came here to get away from … everything."

His eyes widened in horror. She could see the pieces all clicking in his mind as it came together. "Bo and Gwen. Your boyfriend and your best—" He cut himself off. "When I read about it, it felt like one of those nighttime drama story lines, not something real, but obviously, you're real."

"Very much so," she said.

Bennett pointed at Haydn and Jules and said, slowly, "How long have you two known?"

"Earlier today," Haydn said, then tilted his head. Almost as if he didn't mean for it to happen, their gazes collided, and it held her captive. Had she thought this room was cozy? It was sweltering. Whew.

"I've known since that first day, when we were sitting around and drinking hot chocolate. She smiled, and it clicked," Jules said.

Lia and Haydn both turned to him in shock.

"Because of her smile?" Bennett asked. "How did you see it, and I didn't? Rosie has made me listen to every new Aurelia Halifax album with her the *night* it comes out. We stay up all night and eat road trip snacks, and she kicks me awake if I fall asleep." He turned to Lia with a reassuring smile. "Don't get me wrong; it's not a chore to listen. It's just ... Rosie."

Haydn and Jules both nodded, so apparently they both knew what that meant. And maybe, after a week of hearing Rosie stories and being with the brothers, she understood what he meant too. The warmth of belonging filled her.

Jules continued. "The other lawyer who shares my office space is obsessed." Jules turned to Lia. "The concert you did for VidStream is on a constant loop in her office when she's working. She has her headphones in, but I can still see you on the screen."

"And you?" Bennett turned to Haydn, who pushed out his cheeks. "You don't even listen to country music."

"Lia sings pop too."

"Country that's been remixed for the pop station," Bennett corrected, but he turned to Lia for another aside. "It's all brilliant, of course."

"Thanks," she said.

"She mentioned it to me earlier." Now he wouldn't meet her eyes. And she could see understanding dawning on Jules's and Bennett's faces. That's why Haydn was acting so weird. That's why the vibe had changed. Well, if they could figure out why it had changed so much, she'd love for them to let her know.

"I'm sorry I didn't tell you all sooner." She wished Haydn would look at her again. "I liked being normal for once, I guess. And I didn't know if I could trust you guys yet."

Bennett huffed out a breath. "I get that. But you can trust us, for the record."

"I know." She started to play another one of her less popular songs, and Jules dove into singing it in a semi-decent falsetto that completely broke the tension.

"You know this one too?" Bennett threw his hands up. "It didn't even have a radio release."

"I am a multi-layered man," Jules said before continuing to sing, in a normal voice this time. Bennett joined in enthusiastically, his cheeks bright and pink with excitement, and Lia sang harmony.

Haydn didn't know this song, but she felt his gaze like a caress on her skin as she harmonized with Jules. She didn't want to look at him, afraid he'd look away and break the tenuous connection she felt strung between them.

If singing kept that connection, then she'd sing all night. But eventually she'd have to stop and say goodbye to one of the best weeks of her life.

And one of the best people she'd ever known.

21

*L*ia watched Rosie's boat draw closer to the island, arriving to take her to the airport. She couldn't believe it was time. This week had passed in a blink, yet in such a short time, she'd changed. She wanted more time with this island. With Jules and Bennett. With Haydn—to convince him to take a chance on them.

But time was up, and it was time to go home.

Lia had packed up her belongings, written a note for the brothers thanking them for everything, and slipped out of the cabin before any of them could wake up. Was she a coward for trying to leave without saying goodbye? Maybe, but she'd always hated goodbyes.

While Rosie pulled up to the dock, Lia took out her notebook to jot down a few lyrics about heartache, when she heard a voice call behind her.

"You weren't trying to slip away without saying goodbye, were you?" It was Jules, a stern look on his face, as all three Forrester brothers walked out to greet her: Jules in the front, then Bennett, and Haydn trailing behind like a man facing the judges after a bad performance.

"Uh ..." Her cheeks turned hot. She almost never blushed, but yeah. Skipping out on them really wasn't a good look.

"Come here." Jules pulled her into his muscular hug, lifting her up off her feet as he did so. His hard chest pressed against her cheek. He patted her hair, which was frizzy and wild from keeping it in braids yesterday. She'd pulled them out and let the curls live their best Alaskan life under Bennett's bucket hat. She was definitely wearing it in her next short video.

"Haydn mentioned you might need some IP advice. He didn't give me any details." Jules pulled out one of his business cards and handed it to her. "Let me know if you want to chat or if you need help finding a lawyer close to you."

"Thank you." She tucked the card into her back pocket.

Bennett stood next to Jules, and she stepped happily into his warm, comfortable embrace. Hugging Bennett was like wrapping up in that soft blanket she'd debated sneaking into her bag. He made her feel like a tiny woman, and she knew he'd be a protective bear for the people he loved. He sported a black eye and swollen nose, so at odds with his gentle nature.

Rosie jumped off the boat and walked toward them. Bennett and Jules wrapped their baby sister in a sandwich hug that had her squealing in laughter. "What happened to you?" she asked Bennett.

Lia missed his answer as Haydn walked up to her, his hands in his pockets. The wind tousled his long hair in a way that made her want to stand on her tiptoes and push her fingers through it. She clasped her hands behind her back to keep from touching him.

"So this is it," she said.

"I guess so." To her surprise, he reached out to her for a hug. She couldn't resist tugging at his perfect waist and pulling his body flush with hers. If this was going to be the last time she ever touched him, she was going to go all in. Her face fit right up against his warm neck, right where she could brush her lips against his racing pulse if she thought he wanted her to. Sorrow built up in her until she felt like she might choke on it.

She backed away one step and turned, but his hand hooked on hers, and he drew her back into him. She answered the question burning in his eyes by lifting up her heels to press her mouth to his in a heated kiss. So maybe he wasn't so immune to her after all.

When she pulled back, she caught Rosie staring at them wide-eyed and speechless. Bennett and Jules had the same happy but smug twist to their identical mouths. Those Forrester mouths were irresistible, but there was only one she wished she could press her lips to again and again.

After that, the goodbyes went quickly, and before Lia was ready, she and Rosie were on the ride back to Winterhaven. Homesickness swept through her for a place that was never her home, for people who were never her family. But it felt so *right*.

"So Haydn, huh?"

Lia cleared her throat. "I wish."

Rosie gave Lia a questioning look, but Lia stared out at the water and pretended not to see it. How could she explain something she didn't even understand herself?

Lia watched the island get farther and farther from her, until it disappeared completely on the horizon. She turned forward and let the ocean spray hit her face.

She was ready to face everything she'd run from. She'd slowly let down her armor on that island. Piece by piece, she reconstructed it.

Rosie filled the silence by chatting more about her brothers and then transitioning into her shop. She was working on a new commission for her store, and had been holed up in the backroom until late every night. "The dock is crazy, though. So prepare yourself."

"Is there an event in town?"

"I don't think so," Rosie said. "I haven't had a chance to investigate."

The boat drew closer to the marina in Winterhaven, and even from a distance, Lia could see what she meant. When she'd arrived in Winterhaven, she'd loved how quiet and empty the docks had been. Now they were swarming with people, not unlike the numerous starfish dotting the beach on the Forresters' island.

Light glinted on something. On multiple somethings.

Cameras. Oh no.

22

HAYDN

"You going to mope until we leave?" Jules asked Haydn, kicking at his foot where it hung off his bed.

"Yes." He was pathetic, lying on the bed that Lia had been in. He'd drawn the line at smelling her pillow. So far. Who knew what would happen tonight when he started to *acutely* miss her? Versus just *desperately* missing her.

Bennett and Jules exchanged judgy looks. Let them judge. If this was how Bennett felt after his breakup, no wonder he'd been off for months. And Haydn had thought a weekend getaway with brothers could fix this feeling? How naive he'd been.

"Up and at 'em," Jules said, dragging Haydn's feet until he nearly toppled off the bed.

"Let me be."

"Like you let me be after my breakup?" Bennett asked.

"Or when I didn't make partner?" Jules pointed out.

"Or when I almost lost my business?"

"Or when Hallie cheated on me?"

Haydn groaned and covered his face with his elbow. "I was wrong. I should have left you all alone."

"It's not in you to leave us alone." Bennett sat beside him on the bed. "But now it's our turn to help you."

"Whether you like it or not," Jules said, sounding mildly threatening.

Haydn let his arm drop to his side. His brothers were not going to leave him be. He knew them well enough to know that. "Fine. I'm getting up. I'm moving on. Happy?"

"Nope," Jules said. "This is different. You let a perfectly amazing girl go. We"—he pointed between himself and Bennett—"were dumped."

"She's Aurelia Halifax."

Jules lifted a brow. "And you're Haydn Forrester."

"You know what I mean."

"Nope." Bennett shook his head firmly. "You don't just give up on someone because she's famous or there are logistics to work through. What you two have is real."

"The ball is in her court," Haydn said stubbornly.

"Here he comes with a sports metaphor." Jules leveled him with a raised eyebrow. "Tell me, Haydn, which sport is that referring to?"

Haydn had never watched sports much growing up. He'd preferred adventuring in the forest to playing anything. On the other hand, Jules had excelled in any and all sports. "Um ... basketball?"

Jules made a failed buzzer sound. "Wrong. Tennis."

Bennett shook his head like he was sorely disappointed in Haydn for not knowing that. Sometimes having two brothers could be the biggest pain in the world.

Especially when they both sat beside him on the bed, bumping into his shoulder and yelling clichéd sports metaphors like they were his coach until he agreed to go hiking with them.

*H*aydn knew they must have felt really bad for him, because they hiked out to the old cabin without complaint. And when Bennett asked him a question about the old story, he really should have guessed that something was up.

But his mind was so deeply focused on Lia, he didn't suspect a thing until they were at the cabin, all leaning against the huge rock.

"We know about the job offer from *Nature Adventure Magazine*," Jules said without preamble.

Haydn felt like a glass of ice water had been thrown in his face. "What? How?"

"Mickey Wren told me," Bennett said. "He was in town last week, and when I ran into him at the marina, he mentioned how glad he was that you'd turned their offer down."

Haydn closed his eyes. Mickey was the person he'd recommended they reach out to. He wrote for the Alaskan tourism center, and their paths had crossed plenty of times over the years.

"Why did you turn their offer down, Haydn?" Jules asked in his prosecutor voice.

"Does there have to be a specific reason?" He knew he sounded too defensive, and he tried to moderate his tone a little more. Why were they getting into this? He thought they'd come out here to help him get over Lia, not poke at his career choices. "I wanted to stay here."

"Why?"

"To be by you guys." It took everything in him not to roll his eyes, but he did gather his long hair into a messy ponytail, his irritation evident in every jerky move of his arms. "The *Nature Adventure* job would have me relocate to the lower forty-eight for most of the year."

"So? I live down there," Jules countered.

"And I live right by Rosie, and I keep an eye on her anyway when you're out exploring."

"You guys wouldn't get it." He stood and paced away from them, his frustration rising.

"Get what?" Jules said.

"I need to be here. I need to not leave."

"But why?" Jules pushed again.

"Because I can't be like Dad!" he finally said, loud enough to earn a few angry squawks from birds in the trees over their heads. They flew away with a rustle of branches and trees, leaving behind a weighted, uncomfortable silence. "I'm worried that if I give in to my urge to explore the world, I'll never come back."

"You'd never do that," Bennett said, his eyes wide.

"Dad did."

"And you're nothing like him," Jules said firmly. He stood up as well and moved in front of Haydn. "He used to put so much pressure on you. I hated that he called you the glue of our family, because he did it to take the burden off of himself. If you were the glue, then he was unnecessary."

"If you were the glue, then he was free to leave," Bennett added quietly.

Jules placed his hand on Haydn's shoulder as if to hold him in place, which made him pause. Bennett was the huggy-touchy one of them, but for Jules to reach out, it was serious.

"You are a lot like Dad," Jules admitted. The exhaustion lines around his eyes deepened. "He had such a sense of adventure. He's the reason we love hiking and fishing and exploring and boating. Most of our favorite things come from him taking us to do it when we were little. He traveled a lot for work, and I often got the sense that while he was home, he was always waiting for the next trip. That the work trips were his real life, and we were the people and things keeping him from living it. And then Mom got sick, and he got even more restless ..."

Haydn's shoulders deflated, and Jules's hand dropped to his side. He remembered how distant their already-disconnected dad had become once their mom's illness became serious. "I saw Dad the night he left."

Jules's gaze sharpened on Haydn. "I didn't know that."

"I don't know how I realized he was leaving for good. Maybe it was because he had two bags instead of one. Or because he brought both of his favorite guns with him, instead of leaving one home like he always had before. But I raced after him, grabbed him by the back of the shirt, and I told him to mature up and stay."

The wind rustled through the trees, not as wild as the night before, but still sending a chill across his skin. He imagined his young self, trying to speak like an adult to his dad as they'd stood in the entryway of the house. Haydn on one side of the doorway, his father on the other. His voice had cracked when he'd said "stay"—and he hadn't been able to tell if it was the normal teenage voice cracking, or if it was from emotion.

"Dad told me he was leaving the family in good hands, and that I was already a much better man than him." *Take care of them all*, he'd said as he'd tugged his shirt from Haydn's iron grip and taken his first step down the stairs. He'd pointed at Haydn, like he used to do when he'd lecture them and he didn't want any back talk. *I'm counting on you.*

"And then he left." And they'd only seen him once since then—at their mother's funeral. "I've always wondered if there wasn't something I could have done to stop him from leaving. Something I could have said differently or—"

"It's not the kid's job to convince their parent to stay," Bennett said quietly. Haydn knew that was true, knew he would say the same thing if the situation were reversed, yet it didn't *feel* true when it came to him.

"Why didn't you ever tell us this before?" Jules asked.

Haydn shrugged. It was his burden to carry, not theirs. Even now, he could see how weighed down they were by the reality that he'd been left with so much responsibility at such a young age.

"I'm sorry," Jules said simply. "We love you, Haydn, and we know you'd never leave—even if you moved thousands of miles away—because you are absolutely nothing like Dad in the ways that matter. You always come back to us. Even more, you're the one who makes sure we always come back together. Dad was a loose thread, but the rest of us are continuous, interconnected stitches."

Haydn liked that imagery. One stitch alone wasn't strong enough to hold something securely together, but a bunch of stitches in a tight row could do it. Could he stop thinking of himself as the glue and trust himself? That's what it came down to in the end. Could he really believe he wasn't going to be like his dad?

He couldn't imagine doing to his family what his dad had done. Even when he was traveling for work, they texted and talked on the phone. And when they were annoyed or frustrated with each other, when he had to watch his millionth romcom or basketball game or be thrown into a surprise intervention—ahem—he'd never once thought about leaving it all behind.

Haydn pulled Jules into the kind of hug they rarely did anymore, arms fully around each other, his eyes stinging with tears. Jules held him so tight it was almost hard to breathe, but Haydn was glad for the grounding feeling it gave him. He wanted to believe Jules. Wanted to believe him with everything inside of him.

"How long have you been holding on to this for?"

Haydn chuckled wetly. "Years."

"You're not a leaver. You're a stayer—who loves to travel. And I think you might be perfect for a woman who has to travel all over the world for her job. Just saying."

They were just pulling apart when Bennett was at their side in three large steps, his brawny arms wrapped around the two of them. "I wanted to give you two some space, but space is overrated. This is like my dream come true," Bennett said theatrically, which made the other two laugh until they cried and couldn't catch a breath. It was the kind of emotional release that looked ridiculous but felt amazing.

"So what are you going to do about your *Nature Adventure Magazine*?" Bennett asked after they'd pulled apart and discreetly wiped their faces off on their shirts.

"That ship has sailed." Full-time feature openings were rare at most magazines, and *Nature* was especially competitive. He'd tried not to burn any bridges when he'd turned down the offer, but he knew they'd bristled at the rejection.

"What's the plan, then?" Bennett folded his arms.

"I pitched a feature to *Ridges*. I'm hoping for a three-to-four-page spread about our island—filled with pictures and stories, both historical and present."

"That sounds amazing!" Bennett held out his hand for a high five, and Haydn hoped he didn't notice that his return high five was lackluster.

"What did they say?" Jules said, one eyebrow raised. He'd noticed.

Haydn winced. "I haven't checked yet."

The look his brothers leveled at him was enough to make him squirm. "We're checking right now," Jules declared. "Let's go."

Nerves twisted Haydn's stomach as they hiked to the hill on the island that sometimes got reception. He looked up at the overcast sky. Maybe today would be one of those days where he didn't have any bars. He wouldn't mind one more day of wondering. Tomorrow would be soon enough, right?

Not for Bennett or Jules, apparently. They flanked him from

both the front and behind, as if afraid if they took their eyes off of him, he'd run back to the cabin.

The hike was too short, and when he got there, Bennett and Jules faced him with identical steely gazes and folded arms. "Check your email," Jules said in a tone that wasn't open to argument.

Haydn took a deep breath. He could do this. The worst that could happen was that they'd say no. Then he'd be right where he started—disappointed, but no worse off than before. Yet it felt worse off, because now he wanted something more. And that wanting could be painful.

Without thinking too much more about it, he opened his email and found one from his editor.

Haydn,

Yes, let's do the feature. I love it. Will Aurelia Halifax be featured in it as well? (How in the world do you know her? You've been holding out!) Our social media page views have gone crazy. I'll slot you for November.

Oh no. No, no, no. He clicked into his social media app, but it was taking forever to load.

"They're a crap magazine anyway," Jules said.

"Yeah, you can do so much better than them. They're just holding you back," Bennett added.

Haydn looked up at his brothers. "What are you talking about?"

"They said no, right?" Bennett pointed at his face. "You turned all white."

"They said yes." He shook his phone as if that would help the app open quicker.

"Then why—"

Jules's voice was drowned out by the blood rushing in his ears as he pulled up the *Ridges* page and saw that their latest photo had over a million shares. The photo he'd taken of Lia laying out on the rock. Someone had recognized it as her, and it was being shared far and wide.

Bennett looked over his shoulder and read the caption: "'Just outside of Winterhaven, Alaska, a young woman rests in an island paradise. Photo credit: Haydn Forrester.'" He looked up at Haydn. "Maybe no one recognized her."

Jules pulled the post up on his phone a lot quicker than Haydn had. "Did you see the comments?" They were all variations of people excitedly proclaiming that it was Aurelia Halifax. Haydn's stomach pitched, and he thought he might be sick.

"I'm going to google her," Bennett murmured, pulling out his phone. A moment later, he frowned too. "Guys, every story is about how she's in Winterhaven. How likely is it that the media came out here to spot her?"

Haydn bent over, putting his hands on his knees, panic clawing at his chest in a way he'd never felt before. "After all the drama with Bo and Gwen—very likely." And it was all his fault. He'd sent the picture to his editor. He hadn't thought his editor would post it to social media. He hadn't known that Lia was Aurelia Halifax at the time.

But she'd come here to escape, and he'd just thrust her into the heart of the dragon. She was going to think he'd used her to get ahead, just like so many people had done to her.

His hands shook as he sent off a quick message to his editor: Take the picture down. I don't have permission to share her image.

After that, he started running toward the cabin, and he could hear his brother's footsteps close behind him.

"What are you going to do?" Jules called out after him, sounding more out of breath than Haydn would have expected. Maybe pure adrenaline was pushing through Haydn's veins, but right now, he felt like he could fly.

With steely determination that made him pick up his pace, he called back, "I'm going after her."

LIA

"'Oh no,' what? Did something fall out?" Rose said to Lia, a little too loudly. Could everyone hear them? Were they all looking at the dinghy, spotting her already?

"They can't see me," Lia said. She tugged Bennett's hat lower over her head and zipped up Haydn's jacket all the way to the top, before tucking her hair and chin into it.

"Why not? Who are they? Do they know you? Are you running from something?" Her voice pitched upward in a near-squeal, and she sounded entirely too excited about that last question.

Lia took a deep breath. Here was her first test in trusting someone new ... and it was a softball lob. If Haydn trusted Rose, then Lia trusted Rose.

"I'm Aurelia Halifax," she said.

A beat passed, and she could see in Rose's eyes the minute it clicked. "Oh my gosh. Oh my gosh. I knew I recognized you from somewhere!" The boat veered and then slowed down as she threw her hands up to her mouth and squealed into her cupped palms. "You've been staying with my brothers for a week. You and Haydn—" Her cheeks looked flushed. "I think I need to lie down for a minute to process this."

"Rose. If they see me, they're going to mob me with questions, and I'm not ready for that yet." Panic nipped at Lia's heels at the thought of being thrust into the midst of the bloodthirsty media. She couldn't help but feel like they'd love nothing more than to see her fall spectacularly. She knew that wasn't fair, and that it wasn't true for everyone, but when it was just a mass of cameras and a blur of faces, how was she supposed to tell who was safe and who would misrepresent her without a second thought?

"Sorry. Sorry." Rose opened her water bottle, took a drink, and then dumped the rest of it over her face and chest. Ice cubes bounced off of her and onto the bottom of the dinghy, and she took a deep, bracing breath. "I had a moment there, but I'm recovering. I'm recovered. I'm normal now. Approaching normal." She fanned herself with both hands. The dinghy had come to a complete stop.

"Are they going to notice that we're just sitting out here?"

"Nah. People do it all the time. But these guys have binoculars, so we need to move quick." Her eyes narrowed with determination. "I'm going to maneuver the dinghy so that cruise ship blocks us from view. Keep your back to them in the meantime."

She started the dinghy back up, and within a minute, they had the small cruise ship as coverage. Lia felt her shoulders relax with relief. It was going to be short-lived, and she'd probably get caught out in the end, but it was nice to not be in this alone.

The Forrester siblings were amazing people to have on your side.

"Okay, duck down and sit on the floor. It's wet down there, sorry."

Lia did as requested while Rose leaned over her to open a back panel of the dinghy.

She muttered under her breath as she rifled through it. "Ropes, first-aid kit, tube, preserver ... TARP!" She yanked it out and shook it over the ocean while keeping one eye on the cruise ship's trajectory. They only had seconds left. "It's filthy, but it's all I've got."

"I don't care," Lia said. She folded herself into a ball, and Rose tossed the tarp over her back. It smelled like fish, and grains of sand fell like gritty rain onto her skin and hair. She'd never loved a tarp so much.

She closed her eyes and listened as Rose navigated them closer to the marina. Her heart raced as the dinghy slowed down and then puttered to a stop. This was the moment. If Rose wanted to have her minutes of fame, she'd drive straight up to where all the cameras were, and Lia would be completely vulnerable. She imagined the pictures they'd get of her covered in water and fish and sand, crouched in the bottom of the boat. She shuddered, imagining the headlines.

The boat came to a stop, and then she felt the weight shift as Rose hopped out. The side of it hit wood, and then it came to a still stop, other than the gentle rocking of water beneath her.

"The coast is clear, but be quick," Rose said.

Lia slipped out of the tarp and realized they'd docked right beside a boat. She took Rose's outstretched hand, and before she could even take a full breath, they were inside the boat with the door shut.

"I'm going to batten the hatches," Rose said. She rushed around to every window, shutting it and closing the blinds, while Lia shook sand out of her hair and looked around. Colorful art in various mediums covered every available space. It was chaotic and full of life and worked together with a symmetry Lia never could have imagined without seeing it for herself.

Rose then turned on lights so they weren't in the dark, and double-checked windows before turning to Lia with a fiercely protective expression. "No one saw you. I'm sure of it."

"I really can't thank you enough, Rose."

Rose collapsed onto a couch and flung her hands out to her sides. "*Now* I'm going to lie down and contemplate my life and how Aurelia Halifax knows my name."

Lia took a seat at the table across from the couch as her heart rate gradually slowed to normal. She'd never get used to having no privacy, no matter how many years of fame she experienced.

Rose sat up just as quickly as she'd lain down. "Okay, it's processed. My brothers got to spend the week with you? They're so lucky. What did you think of them? Be honest. I can take it. Jules is a little annoying, right? Kind of know-it-all? But Bennett's a total cinnamon-roll sweetie. And Haydn is, like, the best, which you know, since I saw you kiss. Wait! My brother kissed Aurelia Halifax!" Again, her voice squealed at the end. "Never mind, I'm not done processing." She lay back down with her arm over her eyes.

Lia laughed. She was learning that Rose liked to ask a lot of questions at once, and that she spoke really fast. And she was just as loyal and trustworthy as the other Forresters. How lucky was Lia to have met them—even if things didn't end with Haydn how she'd hoped.

"How did they find out you're here?" Rose asked. "Did they GPS-track you somehow?"

Lia shook her head. "I have no idea. I didn't even have my phone on all week." Bo or Gwen wouldn't have added a tracking app to her phone—that seemed like it would be going too far, even for them. She searched through her bag and pulled out her phone to turn it on.

Rose peeked out the curtains. "There's got to be at least thirty of them out there. This is nuts. Winterhaven hasn't seen this much action since ... ever."

Lia didn't see any new apps, and her location sharing was turned off. She typed her own name into her search engine, and an image popped up. It looked like a screenshot from a social media post from the *Alaskan Ridges Magazine*.

In it, she was lying on her back on a rock, her face in profile, but she knew her fans would have recognized her instantly. Photo credit: Haydn Forrester. Her heart sank.

She clicked over to the *Alaskan Ridges* Instagram page and saw a more recent post, saying that Haydn Forrester would be doing a feature for their magazine later this year, with more pictures in this series. Nearly every comment asked if she'd be in more pictures, and whoever ran the Instagram page was vague and teasing, leading the reader to believe that she probably would be.

So he got the feature. At her expense.

How could she feel both happy and devastated at the same time? Had it all been fake? A lie?

"What? What happened?" Rose asked.

Lia flipped her phone around so Rose could see the original post.

Rose's face went from interested to clouded in seconds, and she threw her hands on her hips with a huff. "Did I say Haydn's my favorite? Because he's the worst. Ugh. Worse than land-locked served halibut." She paced back and forth, shaking her head. "No, no one's that bad. But he's worse than my last commissioned painting, which is saying something, because they wanted me to do a wedding-style painting of their cat and dog as bride and groom. Can you imagine? I wish I couldn't." She shuddered.

Lia understood why Rose had wanted to lie down to process things. Her head felt like it was swimming. It didn't help that Rose's constant state of motion and talking was making her feel dizzy. Yeah, she was going to rest her head for just a minute.

She placed it on the table and tried to practice her deep-breathing exercises.

Could she have been so wrong about a person? Again?

Rose groaned and sat on the floor next to Lia's chair. "Lia, I'm soooo torn, because I want to hate him for you, but I can't. Haydn would *never* do something like this. He'd never use someone to get ahead."

"People can change when it comes to fame." She saw it all the time. She'd once thought Gwen would never betray her, but the minute she'd had the chance to make it big—if she had to stomp on Aurelia to get there—she'd taken it.

"Not Haydn," Rose insisted. "He would tank his career to help someone before he'd ever manipulate them to get ahead. There's got to be an explanation."

"Like what?" Lia was grasping for hope. She wanted to believe Rose. Wanted to believe Haydn wouldn't do this.

"Did he know it was you—Aurelia Halifax and not Lia Hall —when he sent the photo to his publisher? I know that's a long shot, but—"

Lia snatched her phone, hoping despite herself, and scrolled to look at the date of the original picture. It was from five days ago. He'd sent it the day they'd gone to look at the starfish and have a picnic. "I hadn't told him who I was yet." She looked at Rose. "He acted so surprised." Angry, even. Her heart clenched. "He couldn't have been faking that, right?"

"No," Rose said fervently. "He's a terrible actor. Like, the worst. He gets all stiff and awkward and does this weird thing with his hand like he's smoking, but he's never smoked in his life, and he says that's just how he holds his hand, but he doesn't."

She demonstrated the weird hand waving near his mouth, and despite all the stress, Lia giggled. "I didn't see him do that at all." She definitely would have remembered. It was ridiculous.

"See? An honest mistake."

Just as quickly as she'd been giggling, though, her stomach turned to stone. Maybe it had been a mistake, but it was just more evidence of how different their worlds were. How they didn't belong together—no matter how much she wished it were different. "What am I going to do? My flight leaves in two hours." She'd never be able to get out of this marina without being noticed.

"Don't worry. An entire life of scheming and planning has led me to this moment." Rose looked around her boat, and Lia could see her brain whirring. Nerves flooded Lia as a Grinch-like smile spread across Rose's face. Rose turned to assess Lia from head to foot. "How do you feel about really small spaces?"

24

HAYDN

Once Haydn had steady cell service, he kept refreshing his email to see if his editor had sent him a message. Finally, his editor sent him a short email: We took the post down. Do we need to notify our lawyer?

Relief flooded Haydn, but it was short-lived. The post had been shared so many times, it now had a life of its own. Taking down the original wouldn't stop people from knowing she'd come to Winterhaven. It wouldn't keep her from seeing it and thinking that he'd sold her out.

He groaned, a sudden headache pulsing behind his eyes.

Bennett rubbed his shoulders. "It's going to be okay! We're going to make this right!" he shouted.

But then the marina came into view, and Jules abruptly pulled back on the throttle. "That's not good," he muttered, taking in the crowd of people milling about the dock.

"Maybe they're all tourists, here to take in our beloved Winterhaven," Bennett said weakly.

Jules and Haydn both leveled him with a look, before Jules pushed the throttle to full speed and headed in the direction of Rose's boat.

They pulled up alongside it. Her boat was there already, so they got off, and Bennett took it over to his boat on the other side of the marina to tie it up.

Haydn banged on Rose's door. "Rose! Are you there?"

Jules walked around to the other side. "All the windows are shut."

Haydn tried the door, and it slid right open. Rose always forgot to lock her doors, something that made Haydn endlessly nervous, but he was grateful for it right now.

The cabin was dark and unmistakably empty. "She's not here," he called out to Jules.

"Do you think they went to the airport?"

"Maybe." If anyone could successfully sneak Lia past all those reporters, it would be Rosie. His heart warmed with gratitude that Rosie had been with Lia when she'd realized her location had been discovered.

No, not discovered. Revealed by him. He'd doxxed the woman he was falling in love with.

"We need to go find her at the airport," Jules declared. "Let's go."

They ran to Bennett's boat first and yelled for him to grab his truck keys; then they raced to his truck. None of the reporters gave them a second look as they went past them.

"Where are we going?" Bennett asked as they all climbed into Bennett's old truck. Jules scrunched himself into the back seat without complaint.

"The airport," Haydn said, feeling determination rise in him. He had to get there. He had to explain himself and apologize. He couldn't send her off thinking that yet another person had betrayed her ... and right when she was starting to trust again.

"The airport it is!" Bennett's wheels squealed as he took the corner out of the parking lot and got on the road to the airport. He flashed a huge, excited grin at Haydn. "I know this is all very serious, but I feel like I'm in a romantic comedy. That last scene where he has to race to the airport to get the girl!"

Haydn's stomach was a bundle of nerves. In those movies, it always worked out. But he didn't know if he'd be so lucky.

It didn't take long to get to the airport, and they spotted Rose's car in the tiny parking lot right away. Bennett turned into a parking space wildly, and Haydn jumped from the truck before it had fully stopped.

Before he realized that the plane was gone.

More reporters loitered around the airport, chatting with one another like they were all old friends. Anger rushed through him, and it took every ounce of self-control not to approach them.

Rosie came out of the trailer, her arms folded and a sour expression on her face. She stomped toward Haydn, but all he could do was watch the plane as it rose into the sky, completely out of reach.

Rosie shoved his shoulder. "What is wrong with you? Why'd it take you so long to get here? I stalled for as long as I could."

"We came as fast as we could," he defended. "Wait, how did you know we were coming?"

She rolled her eyes. "Of course you were coming! This is the airport-chase scene."

"Right?" Bennett said, and the two high-fived.

"I liked the 'squealing into the parking lot' move. That was a nice touch," Rosie said. "I could hear it all the way in the trailer."

Their teasing conversation faded as Haydn's heart sank. He'd been too slow. He'd missed her. Why did it take losing someone to realize how much you wanted them in your life?

He wished he could go back in time, to the conversation they'd had around the seals' shell pile, and react differently to her telling him who she was. He'd pull her into his arms and kiss her like he'd never let her go. Let her decide if they could be together, instead of pushing her away before she could reject him first.

Rosie took his arm in hers and dragged him farther away from the reporters, so they were well out of hearing distance. Haydn turned his back to them. He didn't think they'd recognize him from his profile picture, but these internet sleuths were intense.

"Let's get in the truck," Bennett said.

They all eyed his tiny truck, and Rosie shook her head. "We're taking mine."

~

They picked up some takeout—even though Haydn's stomach was churning too much to eat—and took it back to Rosie's shop. It was closed for the day, so they would have all the privacy they needed to talk. She moved a few things off her art table, and they sat around it with their burgers.

Rosie didn't waste any time. "Well, you botched the romantic gesture—big shocker—so we'd better start thinking of another one."

"Is there another plane going out today?" Bennett asked.

Jules shook his head. "I checked before we left the airport. That was the last one today. The next flight isn't until tomorrow. And even if we got in the boat right now and headed over to Ketchikan, we'd miss the next one out there too."

"I just googled her address," Bennett said, looking up from his phone. "I can't find an exact address—she must have bought it under some sort of company name—but she's definitely in Nashville. And they have those tours that show you where people live. We fly out there, hire one, and show up at her house."

Haydn looked at him incredulously. "No, Bennett. That's so creepy."

"It's romantic," he argued.

"To basically stalk someone?"

"I agree with Haydn," Rosie said, putting an end to that line of thought. "We've got to do something different. Something with more finesse." Her voice drifted off, and he could see her thinking. He'd never been so grateful for his evil genius sister. Which, speaking of ...

"How did you manage to get Lia to the airport without being seen?" he asked her.

"Oh." Her cheeks turned slightly pink. "Well, I stuffed her in my rolling art case. I use it for bigger commissions. Then I just rolled it up to the parking lot and used my ramp to put her in the back of my truck."

"She rode in a suitcase in the back of your truck all the way to the airport?" Jules barked.

"Yep. And then into the airport's trailer too."

Haydn groaned. This was so bad.

Rosie continued. "Mary Anne was working the desk, so I told her what was up, and she rolled Aurelia to the back room to check her in and do her security screen. Then they covered her as she got on the plane. No one saw a thing."

"Where's your case?" Bennett asked.

"Mary Anne's going to drop it off tonight. She was very excited about Lia, but she promised not to say anything to anyone."

Of all Rosie's friends, Haydn was glad Mary Anne was the one working the airport today. She had a steady head on her shoulders and had always been a stabilizing influence in Rosie's life. If she said she'd keep it quiet, he believed her.

"So what's the plan, Rosie?" Bennett asked.

Rosie turned to Haydn. "I have a plan. But I need you to answer one question first. How do you feel about Lia?"

Haydn felt his face heat up, but there was only one answer to this. "I know it doesn't make sense, and we've only known each other for a short amount of time, but I think I love her."

Rosie clapped her hands together and held them under her chin. "Good. Because I think she loves you too. She was devastated when she thought you'd sold her out."

"Maybe she won't even want to see me, then."

"Oh, she'll want to see you," Rosie said. "Trust me."

"There's a flight heading out tomorrow," Jules said. "It'll take us two days to get to Nashville."

"Us?" Haydn said. "You guys are coming with me?"

"Heck yes," Bennett said.

"As if I'd trust you to do this on your own. We saw how well that's been going for you," Rosie deadpanned.

"I still have a few more days off work," Jules said. "It's not every day your brother falls in love with a famous singer."

Haydn felt lighter than he had since the moment he'd walked away from Lia on the island. "Book it, then."

"On it," Jules said.

"I'll work on finding us a place to stay," Bennett said, opening his phone next.

Rosie took his arm and pulled him to sit down beside her on the couch. "And you and me ... we're going to plan the grand gesture of a lifetime."

Haydn didn't know what he'd do without his siblings. He'd had it backwards for so long. He'd thought he was the glue holding them together, but it was the opposite ... they were the glue holding him together.

And right now, he needed them more than ever.

25

LIA

*A*lthough Lia thought she knew what to expect when she arrived home, she was not prepared. To the media, she had fallen off the face of the earth, and she expected to be welcomed home with myriad headlines like "Aurelia Halifax Nurses Broken Heart in Secret." She knew she'd have to face it eventually.

Tomorrow.

Today, she was going to collapse into bed the moment she got home.

Her driver navigated the busy Tennessee traffic, and already Lia was exhausted and ready for another trip to anywhere in the world but here.

Okay, not just anywhere.

Alaska.

With Haydn.

It had taken two days of flights to get home, which gave her a lot of time to think—and she'd come to the conclusion that Haydn hadn't intended to use her to get ahead. The post had been deleted from *Alaska Ridges Magazine*, and she knew that directive could have only come from Haydn.

She'd saved the picture to her phone and looked at it again. It really was an incredible picture. It caught the feel of the island, and he'd captured a moment when she'd been perfectly at peace.

Those two days had also given her time to write. Songs were flowing from her in a way they hadn't since she was still a teenager and writing songs just for fun. These were deeper and fuller and more mature—better than anything she'd ever written. There were some about Haydn—she couldn't deny that—but they were also about the island, and heartbreak, and the abandoned cabin in the woods and their love story, about friendship lost and peace and trust. It was everything she'd experienced in the last couple of months distilled into notes and melodies and lyrics.

It was her heart and soul on a page.

Her back was still feeling kinked from being stuffed in Rosie's case. Rosie drove like the police were on her tail, and Lia still felt every bump from ricocheting from one side of the truck bed to another.

But she hadn't been discovered. She'd made it the entire way home without being recognized. Everyone thought she was still in Winterhaven, so no one expected to see her. Plus she wore sunglasses, Haydn's baggy black hoodie—which she'd stuffed in her backpack before leaving, the first thing she'd ever stolen in her life—no makeup, and her hair split into two frizzy braids.

"Ms. Halifax," her driver said. He stood at the open SUV door. She stumbled up the stairs into her house, and he carried her bag and guitar inside with him before leaving. She locked the door and collapsed into an exhausted, dreamless sleep.

~

*A*n incessant ringing woke Lia up. She groaned when she saw Carmen, her label's PR person, on the phone. It had been so wonderful to not have cell service for a week in Alaska. Her phone had been pinging nonstop since she'd landed in Seattle, but she'd been sending everyone to voicemail … and then deleting their messages un-listened to.

She had one hundred and fifty-six unread texts. Her assistant took care of her emails, so she didn't have to tackle that, at least. But she had to start answering her phone at some point.

"Hello?" she said as pleasantly as she could muster.

"Aurelia," a nasal voice said. "Oh, thank goodness. We thought you'd fallen off the face of the planet."

"Nope. Still here."

"Fallen right off into oblivion," Carmen continued as if Lia hadn't spoken at all.

"I was in Alaska," she said.

"I know, dear. Basically oblivion. Meanwhile, you won't *believe* what happened. Bo and Gwen broke things off. They've been fighting publicly, and Bo swears he's going to win you back. Gwen says she'd never let her best friend be with a lying cheater like him."

"Wait. What?" Lia blinked. Had she woken up in an alternate universe?

"They're spilling each other's secrets left and right."

What about her songs? Had they fessed up to that? She did a quick search, but apparently they were keeping that secret under wraps for now. She pulled out Jules's business card. She could call or text him right now. They were probably off the island, heading home.

Carmen was still talking. "You revealing that you've been hidden out on an island with a mystery man has been stealing their thunder. Brilliant move, Aurelia."

"Wait, what are they saying?"

"Have you not been following any of this?" she huffed.

"I didn't have cell service on the island." And she hadn't been ready to face reality yet for the last couple of days.

"Your fans. They're going wild about you and Henry."

"Haydn."

"Sure, whatever. They're trying to figure out who he is and how you met and if you're getting married. I saw his picture … and wow, if that's the kind of man hiding out in Alaska, book me a trip."

"What picture?" She was googling frantically, but all she was coming up with were Gwen and Bo and that same picture of Lia on the island, over and over again, with different commentary each time.

"It looks like he's on a mountain somewhere. And there's another one of him swimming. It's all over the fan pages."

She clicked over to social media and searched up her fan pages. She never followed any of these—it was either people so in love with her it made her uncomfortable, or it was filled with people who hated her intensely and argued with everyone who posted about how much they loved her songs. She'd learned early on to stay away from those pages to preserve her own sanity.

Now, she scoured them like a thirteen-year-old mega fan, searching for any new information. And there he was. Her heart skipped when she came across the photo of Haydn swimming in a lake. The water was a deep blue, and with the snow-capped mountains behind him, she imagined it was freezing cold. You could only see him from the waist up, and he was laughing, his eyes focused on someone off camera.

She missed him so much it hurt.

"Are you even listening, Lia?"

Lia blinked a few times. "I've got to go," she said, and she hung up while Carmen was yelling at her to stay on the phone.

But her brain was too full of Haydn. She scrolled through several more posts where people had dug out pictures of him. Her heart ached looking at them, but she couldn't stop. Someone had linked the *Alaska Ridges Magazine* website, and she clicked on it.

From there, she searched out his name and spent hours looking at pictures he'd taken. He really was incredible. He had a way of capturing movement that made you feel like you were there. His mastery of light and dark was stunning. And the colors of Alaska were in every brilliant shade of the rainbow. It made her homesick for a place she'd only visited. For a person she'd only known for a week.

She needed someone she could talk to about this.

Who do you have? It was a question she'd asked herself on a loop since Haydn had brought it up. She could call her assistant, and she'd listen and offer sympathy, but Lia wanted someone who wasn't on her payroll. Someone she could trust fully.

She picked up her phone and scrolled through it until she arrived at her dad. What would happen if she called? It was a Saturday. He usually didn't work on Saturdays.

She held her breath and pressed the send button with shaking fingers.

He answered it on the first ring. "Lia!" She imagined the smile on his face—he was always quick to smile. "We were just talking about you."

"You were?"

"Yeah. The kids were asking when you're coming to see us again."

"Oh." She hadn't expected this. Sure, they'd made her feel welcome last time she'd come—but her siblings didn't care that she was famous, and her stepmom always seemed to be trying a little too hard. She often wondered if they were relieved when she left. "Um, I don't know. I'll have to check my schedule."

"Okay."

They were both silent for a moment, and she could hear her half-siblings in the background talking to their mom.

Her dad said, "Well, it was good to hear from you," and she recognized the beginnings of closing a phone call.

"Wait, Dad. Do you have a minute ... to talk?"

"Oh." He sounded surprised. "Sure. Let me just get into my office. Hang on." She heard him moving around, and the sounds got quieter. "What's going on?"

"I don't know where to start." To her mortification, though, she started to cry. She hadn't cried once since leaving Alaska, but now it all came pouring out of her in one huge rush.

"Is this about Bo?" he asked quietly.

"You know about that?"

"Everyone knows about it. Marissa wants to send him a bouquet of dead flowers."

Lia laughed through her sniffles. "I'm sorry. I didn't mean to call you to cry. I just ... I just needed someone I could talk to. Who won't sell me out to the press."

"Then it sounds like you came to the right person. What's going on?"

Lia filled him in on everything, starting with Bo and Gwen and finishing up kissing Haydn and then being rolled into airport security in an art case. At one point, she heard Marissa come into his office, but he told her he'd have to meet them wherever they were heading, and he kept on listening.

Warmth rushed through her at the realization that she was talking to someone. Trusting them. And it didn't really matter what her dad said, if he had good advice or not. What she really needed to know was that he cared about her.

"It sounds like you need a good old-fashioned family dinner."

"Dad." She laughed wetly. It was something he used to say when she was growing up, whenever she'd had a hard day at school. What she wouldn't give for one of her dad's overcooked hamburgers. "As much as I'd love that, I just got home. I can't get away again."

"Then we'll come to you. The kids are off for summer, Marissa is due a few weeks off of work, and it's been years since I brought everyone to Nashville."

As much as she'd love to see him, she remembered why they'd stopped coming to see her. The attention from the press could be overwhelming, and she couldn't go anywhere with them without making the whole trip miserable. "That's okay, Dad. I've got a benefit concert next weekend, but maybe I can get away for a few days after that."

"I'm already looking at plane tickets. Where's the concert? I'll grab tickets for that too."

"The concert is sold out, but I can get you guys some tickets in the front." She paused. "Are you sure?"

"Yes," he said, sounding serious. "I wish I would have known all of this sooner, Lia. I'm here for you, okay. Even if I'm all the way in North Carolina. I know I get busy sometimes, but I'm never too busy for you."

There were those darn tears again. She blinked them back and said, "Okay. I love you."

"Love you too." It had been a while since she'd heard that phrase and believed the person meant it. It was nice. More than nice. Essential.

She ended the call, feeling just as much peace as she'd felt out on the Forresters' island. It really was good to have people on her side.

26

HAYDN

"Oh my gosh, Haydn. What did you do?" Rosie was sprawled across his bed, in the hotel room he was sharing with Bennett, scrolling through her phone. Nashville was a lot more humid that he'd expected, and he'd moved to the seat right next to the air conditioner.

"What?" he asked.

She sat up straight, still scrolling. "Please tell me you didn't comment on her fan page. Wait, no. Multiple fan pages?"

He winced guiltily. "Jules thought it might be a good idea—"

"This is why you have me!" She closed her eyes and groaned. "This is so cringe, Haydn. I'm dying of secondhand embarrassment right now. We might have to call the whole thing off."

Haydn was used to Rosie's theatrics, but since he was already nervous about tonight, her words were putting him on edge more than they usually would. "Why?" He pulled up his own phone to look up some of the comments he'd made. He and Jules thought they were a perfect blend of casual and inconspicuous, while still aiming to get her attention, when they'd written them together last night after the group had split into their hotel rooms—Bennett and Rosie in one, Haydn and Jules in the other.

She let out a short breath, as if grasping for patience. "Tell me. Do you really think she runs her fan pages?"

"No, she has people that do that for her, but we figured they could pass the message along."

"You and Jules figured that, did you?" She blinked at him a few times, and he felt the sweat building up behind his collar. Jules and Bennett had left to go pick up food while Haydn rested for the big night. But rest was impossible.

Lia's benefit concert was tonight, and he was going to shoot his shot as soon as it was over. Tickets had been sold out for months, but they'd purchased some online from a reseller for about ten times the normal value. No one had batted an eye at the price, so he tried not to either as he'd pressed the purchase button.

But thinking about attempting to talk to her after the concert—there was a small mix and mingle for people willing to spend enough money to buy another tiny island in Alaska (he was such a person, apparently)—made it impossible to rest or to get comfortable. Why was Nashville so hot? He couldn't *think* in this heat.

"You and Jules believe she runs sites called AureliaHalifax-BiggestFan05 and ILoveAH4Ever?"

He wouldn't tell her about the other ten or so he and Jules had posted on. Didn't seem like the time. "I thought so, yes, but now I'm second-guessing." Did he sound frustrated? Yes. Did he care? No. He jammed his finger on the lower temperature button for the A/C. He wasn't paying the electric bill in this place.

Rosie tossed her phone to her side and threw herself back

on the bed. "My brothers are idiots. It's amazing they managed to survive this long without me." She sat up then and leveled him with a glare. "They're run by fans, Haydn. Hardcore, name their kids after her, tattoo her name on their chest fans. She has nothing to do with these sites, and I guarantee you she never looks at them."

"Oh." Whoops.

"Yeah. And you're all up in them writing things like ..." She lowered her voice. "'Lia, I wish we could go back and have "a pleasant walk, a pleasant talk, along the briny beach." Miss you. H.'"

"It's from 'The Walrus and the Carpenter.'"

"I know," she said slowly. "And so does everyone else, because they've looked it up. You know what else they know? What H stands for, because you used your own profile to comment. It's all over social media."

"Are you serious?" Embarrassment made him feel even hotter. He'd never intended for anyone to see those comments—or think twice about them—other than whoever ran the fan sites. They'd send the personal message to Lia, she'd see it, and she'd know that he was referring to that last day on the beach when she'd told him who she was. That he regretted pushing her away. That he missed her.

"People are tweeting it and subtweeting it and making whole boards about it, and someone even has a dedicated page to it now." She went silent for a minute as she looked at her phone. "Oh, no. This is bad, so bad."

He felt his energy drain out of him . "Do I even want to know?"

"How many followers did you have on Instagram last week?"

He rarely checked his Instagram, except to add photos maybe once a week. "Maybe five thousand."

She looked up at him, and by the ill expression on her face, he knew. "You now have *twenty*-five thousand. Don't you get notifications?"

"No. I turned them off years ago." He stared up at the ceiling. Rosie was right. They might have to call the whole thing off. It looked like he was still using her to get more followers. She would never listen to him now.

He went to his Instagram and closed down his account, but the damage was probably already done. He'd also quit his job with *Alaska Ridges Magazine*. He didn't want to have association with anything that could tie any success of his with Lia. He had to prove to her that he would never use her. That he loved her. And maybe she'd look at him like he was crazy. Laugh. Remind him that they were just as summer fling. But he hoped she wouldn't, and that hope was what had brought him and his siblings this far.

"Wait, what did you do?" Rosie said, sounding frantic. "I can't access your Instagram anymore."

"I closed my account."

"What? You can't get followers like that again!" Was it possible for Rosie to look any more stressed? "Okay, from this moment on, you are not allowed to make any moves without me." She closed her eyes and took a few deep breaths. He remembered her learning how to do meditative breathing after their mom died, to help her with the panic attacks she'd been plagued with for months. "I'm good. Actually, that was the right move, to delete it. I was thinking with my Instagram influencer brain and not my romantic brain. Rookie mistake."

"I'm sorry, Rosie. I know I've botched this, but we're doing it."

She nodded forcefully. "Yes, we are. At least she's going to know what a goober she's agreeing to be in a relationship with. No unpleasant surprises later."

"See? There's the silver lining."

She held up her finger menacingly. "Don't push it. No more going rogue. Stick to the plan."

He held up his hand. "I promise."

The hotel door opened, and Bennett and Jules walked in with their food, happily chatting. Until Rosie stood up and approached Jules with a threatening glare. "Jules, a word please?"

Haydn was glad he wasn't his brother.

~

The concert was so much more packed than he'd anticipated. They found their seats in the bottom bowl of the arena, about thirty rows back from the stage. The crowd was energized. Haydn didn't know if the feelings rolling through him were nerves or excitement.

He couldn't wait to see Lia, even if this was as close as he ever got. He'd listened to her songs nonstop since deciding to come out to Nashville, and he knew them as well as Jules did now. She was brilliant, and the thought of her ex stealing her songs made him even angrier. How could people not hear it? He'd streamed Gwen's songs one time, just to hear Lia's lyrics, and he could tell it was Lia's work with every turn of phrase. She had a way of saying so much with so few words and managed to evoke images and emotion in a tiny space. What he tried to do with his photos, she was already doing with her songs. It was no wonder she was so beloved.

He had been secretly hoping she'd look out in the crowd and notice him before she got on stage, but as he looked at the thousands of people surrounding him, he knew it was a long shot.

More than a long shot. It was never going to happen.

The lights lowered, and brilliant stage lights turned on. Everyone cheered wildly, and he found himself caught up in the energy of the crowd. Soon, he was cheering and whistling just as loud as everyone else as the stage changed colors from blue to purple to pink to orange and then to yellow before finally landing on a dark red, the color of the charity she was singing for tonight.

The first notes of her most popular song, "Unsteady in Love," started to play, and the crowd went even wilder. When she finally stepped out on stage, Haydn's heart stopped. He'd still been picturing Lia on the beach—with her hair in two braids, no makeup, her nose a little sunburned and pink, wearing his oversized clothes. Here, on stage, was a Lia that took his breath away. She wore a flowing blue-green gown—the color of the ocean waves on a peaceful day. Her hair had been curled and left to flow around her shoulders. Her lips were a kissable cherry red, and every part of her was Aurelia Halifax.

Was he really going to make a play for Aurelia Halifax?

Yes, he was. Because even though the woman on this stage might never once have looked twice at Haydn Forrester, Lia Hall did. And when she finished singing the song, and the crowd lost themselves in cheering, and she sat on a stool someone had set on the stage to stare out at the crowd, all he could see were Lia's eyes.

"Hi, everyone! I'm so glad to be here tonight." She laughed as everyone's cheers interrupted her. He was immediately transported back to walking along the island trails with her, craving that laugh so deeply. "We've got a fun night tonight, and I'm going to play some of my hits for you, but I wondered ... who here wants a sneak peak of my new album coming out soon?"

If he thought the crowd had cheered loudly before, he was wrong, so wrong, because this reached the kind of decibel levels that would have his ears ringing for days.

She laughed again, and someone brought out her guitar. He recognized it from the house. She ran her fingers over the strings and started to play chords that sounded familiar. The notes she'd been playing with on their way to the abandoned cabin. "Some of you may know I went to Alaska for a secret getaway—"

More cheers. It had been all over the news for the last week.

She continued to play the guitar while she spoke. "And while I was there, I visited an old cabin that had been owned by a man who pined for his lost family his entire life. It was heartbreaking, but also inspiring. A love like that—it seemed so essential. So rare. I wrote this song for him. It's called 'The Light.'"

She started to sing then, about love and longing and a man who still searched for his family, and the words hit him to the very core. She'd managed to capture the essence of his favorite story—he could picture the man wandering the island with his fading light shining across the waterway.

Rosie took his arm and rested her head on his shoulder. He looked down and saw that she was crying. His brothers reached out and patted his back and shook his free shoulder. They all knew what this story meant to him, and how it felt to hear Lia honoring it in such a perfect way.

If he hadn't been in love with her before, he was one hundred percent fully in love with her now. He didn't care that they'd only known each other a week. Or that they lived two very different lives. Or that he'd messed this up in every way possible. Every reservation he had was laid to rest as he heard her sing this song. All his nerves fled, and in their place was determination.

She finished the song, and there was a beat of silence before everyone started cheering and screaming. Haydn wasn't going to have a voice at the end of this to declare his love with, if he wasn't careful.

"Lia!" Rosie screamed. "Haydn's here! Haydn's here!"

Haydn shot a quick look over at his sister, who had tears

streaming down her cheeks. What in the world was she doing? This was *not* the plan.

"Haydn's here!" she kept screaming at the top of her lungs, her hands around her mouth to amplify the sound. The people sitting around them started to turn around and look at him.

Some of them whispered, and then someone leaned forward to say, "Hey, are you that guy she was in Alaska with? Haydn Forrester?"

"Yes, it's him," Jules said. He shrugged at Haydn, then started yelling, "Haydn's here!" as well.

"This is the guy from the fan page comments!" another person yelled. "The Alaska guy."

Soon the people around them all joined in, and whispers began to spread in the area around them. The chant picked up speed, everyone pointing in his direction as they screamed his name for Lia.

He didn't know if he should hide his face or climb on his chair so she could see him. "Rosie, I don't want to ruin her moment."

"Oh, just go with it, Haydn. This *is* her moment! Look!"

He did, and he realized that Lia had stopped talking. The chants of "Haydn's here" had grown louder and louder, and she blinked a few times and then took her earpieces out. She looked down at someone near the front row, her expression unsure. Then she looked out at the crowd, in the direction everyone was pointing in.

"Haydn's here!"

"Stand on the chair, you doofus," Rosie said, trying to manhandle him up onto his seat. And he'd learned long ago that one did not ignore Rosie Forrester. So he stood on the chair and felt the moment Lia's eyes met his across the floor.

Everyone else saw it too, because their chanting for him erupted into wild screams and whistles.

"Well," she said into the mic, a small smile playing at the corner of her lips. "If it isn't Haydn Forrester."

Hearing his name come from her mouth made his heart race. He knew she'd never hear anything he said, so he waved like a windshield wiper clearing gunk of the glass.

"Hi, Haydn." She laughed, and her eyes sparkled like she might be as excited to see him as he was to see her. A tightness in his chest unfurled.

"You are so awkward," Rosie hissed. "Do something!"

"Like what?" he hissed back.

"Anything!"

So he made a heart with his hands.

Rosie shrieked and pulled his arm down. "Anything but that. This is so embarrassing."

But all around them, other people were making hearts with their hands as well, and the cheers were rising again. Lia grinned widely and put her earpiece back in. "Haydn, this one's for you."

She began to play another song, this one about a girl who wants more than a summer fling with a boy who finally sees her for her.

Everyone started nudging him to go forward, and Haydn felt his adventurous spirit spark.

"Go!" Bennett said, pushing his back.

Haydn started to walk down the aisle, toward the stage, and security let him through when Lia waved him up. He went up the stairs and to her side as she finished the song. The final lyric was, "Could he love me too?"

He saw her reach down and turn her mic off.

Haydn couldn't wait a moment longer. He stepped close to Lia, and she closed the gap, crushing her lips to his in the kind of kiss that only happened once in a lifetime. The crowd around them lost their minds, but the sound disappeared until it was only him and Lia on the stage.

He pressed his hands to her back to pull her closer, and her arms went around his neck, her fingers spearing into his hair.

"You taste like sunshine," she murmured against his mouth, sending tingles through his entire body. "I don't know how that's possible."

"I love you," he whispered close to her ear. "Can you forgive me?"

"For what?" She pulled back to take him in.

"Everything. Being so awful when I found out who you are. Giving my editor your photo and accidentally outing that you were in Alaska. Commenting on your fan pages to try to get your attention. The Instagram followers thing. I would never use you to get ahead."

She placed finger over his lips, and he kissed it. "You've been busy." She shook her head. "I don't know half of what you're talking about. But I know you. And I trust you."

"I trust you too."

"What about ... not having space for more people in your life?"

He hated how vulnerable she sounded. That he'd been the one to make her feel that way. "I will always have space for you. You have all the space. It's yours." He rubbed at his heart, knowing he'd never said anything truer.

Her eyes glistened with tears, and she blinked. "Don't make me cry. I still have to sing for another hour."

He pressed his forehead to hers. "I love your new songs. They're my favorites."

"Mine too. That island, Haydn. It was magical. Being with you, your family, in that space. It's changed my life." She paused and cocked her head to the side. "I think they're chanting 'kiss again.'"

"It's like they can read my mind." He wanted nothing more than to kiss her again, forever and ever, but he wanted to make sure she wanted this too.

She stared in his eyes, taking in all of him, all the way to his soul. "I love you, Haydn Forrester." But this time, her mic was on, and it was broadcast to the entire arena. She gave him an impish smile that made his stomach do a somersault, and he angled his head to capture her lips in his again. She tasted like cinnamon and the future.

And he couldn't wait to see what happened next.

27

ONE WEEK LATER:

LIA

The world has lost its mind.

HAYDN

Are you referring to Haydelia? Because my good friend at Aurelia-Halifax-Number-One-Fan coined that term.

Or was it AureliaIsDaBomb?

LIA

How many fan sites did you comment at?

HAYDN

I honestly thought I could reach you that way.

LIA

Well, in a roundabout way, you did.

HAYDN

Jules is taking all the credit for this, by the way. It's driving Rosie nuts.

LIA

Poor Rosie. Tell her she gets ultimate credit for booking me your cabin.

HAYDN

People are loving your new songs. From what I've seen all the way up here in Alaska. Where I'm definitely not stalking you via Google alerts.

LIA

I'm dead. You didn't.

HAYDN

No, but Bennett did for about a day. He set up alerts, went fishing with some clients for eight hours without his cell phone, and when he got back, he had so many alerts he debated deleting his account and starting over.

LIA

Why would he follow me???

HAYDN

That's Bennett. He has your back. He's showing support by knowing what's going on in your life.

We can't all be so privileged as to have your phone number. Like some people.

Like me. I mean me.

LIA

Ha ha. You can give him my number. He can check in any time. Jules too. I trust you guys.

HAYDN

And me?

LIA

You can check in ALL the time.

HAYDN

Good, because I plan to.

LIA

Thanks for crashing my concert.

HAYDN

Anytime.

Just kidding. I hope I'm never on stage again.

LIA

It wasn't so bad, was it?

HAYDN

No, but only because I was with you.

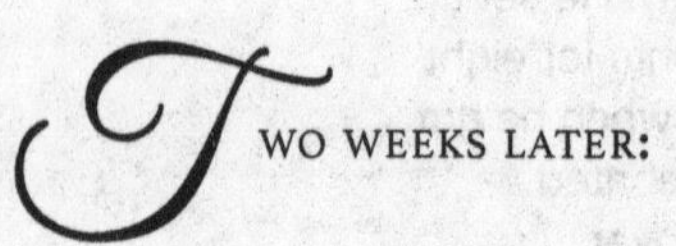WO WEEKS LATER:

LIA

My dad is your biggest fan. He likes you more than me.

HAYDN

Doubtful.

LIA

He just ordered every back issue of Ridges magazine you're in.

HAYDN

Wow. That's really awesome. And kind of terrifying.

LIA

I'm glad you got to meet him.

HAYDN

Me too. Even if meeting him after he saw me kiss you in front of thousands of people was a little awkward. When we came up with our plan, we didn't anticipate your family being in the audience.

LIA

I've seen him kiss Marissa enough times not to worry about it.

It was nice having all the people I loved there.

HAYDN

SAME.

But heads up—I'm pretty sure Marissa and Rosie exchanged numbers. They were talking about ordering dead flowers ...?

LIA

Uh oh. Those two are a revenge duo made in heaven.

ONE MONTH LATER:

HAYDN

You'll never guess what I did today?

LIA

Write a new chapter of your book?

HAYDN

Well, yes. But I also got to remove a fishing hook from someone.

LIA

Where?

HAYDN

On his gluteus maximus.

LIA

Hahahaha! I meant where did this happen?

HAYDN

That makes more sense. I was in Sitka, interviewing some old fishermen for my book and taking photos.

LIA

And they had *you* remove it?

HAYDN

Rite of passage or something. I had to prove myself before they'd talk to me.

LIA

Ooookay.

HAYDN

At-home glute piercings. They're all the rage.

LIA

Hopefully that trend doesn't come to Nashville.

HAYDN

Oh, I don't know. It might not be so bad for my newly acquired hook-removing skills to be needed there.

LIA

True. I like the way you think.

HAYDN

How's your new song going?

LIA

SO good. I started working with Mikela Jarrod and she's brilliant. The layers she's bringing to this song … I can't wait for you to hear it.

HAYDN

I'm sure it's going to be amazing.

~

LIA

It's done! *collapses*

HAYDN

The song? You recorded it?

LIA

I just got home from being in the studio for NINE hours. I'm never getting up from this couch again.

HAYDN

I want to hear it.

LIA

I sang it for you last night.

HAYDN

Video chat isn't the same.

LIA

As hearing a recording?

HAYDN

No. Being in person together.

LIA

AGREED.

HAYDN

What if I come to Tennessee again? I have so many stories and pictures collected, I could use some down time to pull it all together.

LIA

Yes. When?

HAYDN

I'm looking now... next week?

LIA

Perfect.

HAYDN

Just a sec. I'm getting a call...

LIA. That was the agent I've been working with. A publisher is interested in my book! They love the idea of me pulling together the stories of different people I've met in Alaska, and they love my photos too. They want me to have a rough draft to them by January.

LIA

YAY!!!!! Congrats! This is so well-deserved. Are they going to let you have a chapter on the island?

HAYDN

Yes. Holy cow. I think I'm in shock.

LIA

It's going to be amazing.

I'm calling you.

~

FOUR MONTHS LATER:

BENNETT

I heard your song on the radio!!!!!!

It's soooooo good. I can't believe I know you.

LIA

Thanks, Ben.

BENNETT

I didn't think it could get any better than when you sang it at the concert, but you're magic.

LIA

The island is magic. I just happened to be lucky enough to get inspired while I was there.

BENNETT

Tell Haydn I said hello!

Ever since he got to Tennessee he hasn't been returning my texts. It's like he's busy or something :) Are you two having fun?

LIA

Eh, it's okay, I guess.

Hahahaha, just kidding. Haydn was reading over my shoulder and I was messing with him. I'm having the best time with him here. The Best.

FIVE MONTHS LATER:

LIA

It wasn't long enough.

HAYDN

It never is. Leaving you was nearly impossible.

LIA

Watching you leave was just as impossible.

HAYDN

Why do I live in Alaska, again?

LIA

Because that's where your family is. And you need to finish your book there.

HAYDN

I'm almost done with my book.

And my family needs an excuse to come to Nashville more often.

I love you, Lia. I don't want to keep leaving you.

LIA

I hate when you leave too.

Maybe someday we'll be in the same place for more than a couple of weeks.

Oh, and my dad says hi. He read your guest feature in Nature Adventure Magazine, and he's been bragging about knowing you to all his friends.

HAYDN

Well, that's not embarrassing at all.

LIA

You're kind of a big deal, Haydn.

HAYDN

I'm never going to live that down.

Six Months Later:

HAYDN

Tomorrow, tomorrow!

LIA

Did I ever tell you I played Annie in my community theater in sixth grade? I wore a red wig.

HAYDN

I love that. I must see a picture.

LIA

I'll see if I can dig one up. I'm surprised you know the reference.

HAYDN

Before Rosie made us watch romcoms, she made us watch musicals.

LIA

Ah, I should have guessed.

I'm all packed and ready to leave in the morning. My driver is coming at five am.

HAYDN

Are you sure you can get away? I can't WAIT to see you, but I know Carmen is freaking out.

LIA

Carmen was born freaking out. She'll be fine. I won't be off the grid this time.

I'm not even there yet, and I wish I could stay longer.

HAYDN

Me too.

LIA

Do I look Alaskan ready? *picture of her wearing a black oversized hoodie and Bennett's fishing hat*

HAYDN

Wait. Is that … is that my hoodie?

LIA

What? This old thing? I've had it for at least six months …

HAYDN

It looks way better on you than it ever looked on me.

LIA

I'm sorry I stole it.

Also, I'm not sorry at all.

HAYDN

I can seriously picture your impish smile right now. And tomorrow, I get to see it in person.

~

 NE YEAR LATER:

HAYDN

WAKE UP!

BENNETT

Dude.

JULES

It's four in the morning.

HAYDN

And it's MOVING day!

JULES

Is he like this when he's out interviewing people?

BENNETT

Insufferably perky?

JULES

At unholy hours of the morning.

BENNETT

You used to hate mornings, Haydn. Remember that?

JULES

Ah, the good ol' days.

ROSIE

You guys are just jealous. Haydn's happy and moving to Nashville to be near his girlfriend, while you two are losers.

HAYDN

Ahem … one small correction.

Fiancée. Not girlfriend.

ROSIE

She hasn't said yes yet.

BENNETT

She will.

JULES

I'm surprised SHE hasn't proposed yet. It's been a year, Haydn.

HAYDN

Since we MET. We wanted to take things slow.

BENNETT

I think it's nice that you two didn't rush things. You both had stuff to work through.

ROSIE

Blah, blah, blah.

When you guys added me to your text chat, I thought it was going to be juicy. But all you do is complain about each other and talk about your feelings.

JULES

Alright. I'm awake. Even though I don't need to be because I'm flying to Nashville from Seattle and not ALASKA.

JULES

But I'm feeling really connected to my inner self today. My irritated inner self.

BENNETT

I feel that you're feeling that, Jules. And I'm
feeling all the rest of the feels.

HAYDN

Let's analyze all those feels, guys. Let it out.

ROSIE

UGH! I'm texting Lia.

Aurelia Halifax is going to be my sister-in-
law. Eep!

28

HAYDN

Haydn had dropped Bennett and Rosie off at the hotel, and Jules was arriving in a few hours, but Haydn couldn't wait one more moment to see Lia.

He'd texted her to say he was in town, and she'd sent him the address to her recording studio.

He liked the rental truck he drove to get to her. Maybe he'd get one just like it. He'd sold most of his belongings when he'd decided to move to Nashville, and he had been living with Bennett for the last three weeks.

He'd finished his book, and it was heading to print soon. He was already working with his agent on another book idea, and he'd agreed to write a regular feature for *Nature Adventure Magazine*. They'd agreed to let him have his home base in Nashville, especially since he would be traveling the world as a photographer for them.

After he submitted his finished book, things moved quickly. He sold his car. His boat. Said goodbye to his friends. And counted down the seconds until he could be with Lia.

They talked on the phone almost every day. And if they weren't talking, they were texting or video chatting or sending video messages. His every waking moment revolved around someone who lived over three thousand miles away from him.

And now, he'd be able to see her in person. More than just once a month when they managed to travel back and forth from Nashville to Alaska. Lia's album had exploded in sales, earning her a number one spot on the charts, and had become a crossover hit on the pop station.

He found a parking space and walked into the studio. Lia was waiting for him in the doorway. Her hair was in braids, the same way she'd worn it in Alaska. Her cheeks were bright pink, something he'd learned happened when she'd been recording. The heat in the studio, combined with her full concentration on her music, made her cheeks heat up.

"Haydn!" She ran to him, and he hauled her into his arms and spun her around.

"I missed you," he said.

"Me too. But I'm here for good now." She grabbed his cheeks and pulled him in for a kiss that he fell into completely.

Lia was everything. She was nature hikes and sunny afternoons. She was gorgeous melodies and poetic lyrics. She was laughter and joy and thought and fate.

Wherever Lia was, she was his home.

He was going to pick up the ring this afternoon. Ask her if she wanted to spend an entire lifetime with him.

And he could hardly wait.

29

LIA

Lia had arranged for Haydn and his siblings to be in the front row of her concert on opening night. Her dad and his family were there too. They were all coming back to her place for a late dinner after the concert—her stomach was too excited to eat anything too substantial before she got on stage.

The opening act, a young girl who reminded her a lot of herself at that age, was singing a few cover songs and getting ready to launch into her brand-new single. Crew ran around backstage in a frenzy, while Lia practiced some deep-breathing exercises she liked to do before she performed.

She was having a hard time getting into a zen headspace, though. Because she'd seen the ring box in Haydn's jacket. He didn't know she'd seen it, but when she'd hugged him earlier, his pocket had fallen open and the small, square velvet box had been unmistakable. She'd wanted to snatch it open right at that moment and slip the ring on her finger. Wear it for everyone to see at her concert, and announce to the world that she was marrying Haydn Forrester.

The crowd cheered as the young artist sang her single.

"Ready, Aurelia?" Her pianist stood beside her, a wide, excited smile on her face.

"Absolutely. Did you have a chance to play through that song I sent you?" Haydn thought he was surprising her, but Lia had something up her sleeve too.

"I did." She laughed and shook her head. "This is epic."

The lights went down, and Lia's intro music began. She ran to get into place and headed on stage. The crowd went wild, and she waved and smiled and searched for the one person she most wanted to see: Haydn, in the front row, with that familiar smile just for her.

She curled her fingers into a heart, and he returned the symbol to her. She'd thought it was adorable when he'd done that at her last concert. If she'd thought everyone went wild earlier, she'd had no idea.

The concert passed in a blur, starting with her old songs and then moving on to her new ones. Before she got to the songs she'd written while on the island, she paused to speak to everyone.

"There's one song I haven't shared with anyone yet. It's a very special song to me. The first one I wrote when I got to Alaska. I was in a really bad place—reeling from betrayals and heartbreak and feeling like I might never be able to write again."

She'd won her intellectual property lawsuit against Gwen and Bo, and the world knew about it. Their careers had faded into oblivion over the last year, and last she'd heard, they'd moved to California. She didn't wish them any ill will, but she also wasn't sad that she wouldn't be running into them unexpectedly anywhere.

"And in the middle of all that, I was on the worst airplane trip I'd ever been on. This tiny plane was all over the place. People were screaming and crying, cups were flying, and I was sincerely regretting that I'd packed my guitar under the plane. I needed something to hug."

She pulled her guitar close and hugged it, which caused a mixed reaction of laughing and aww-ing.

"I was desperately trying to think of a new song to distract myself, when the handsomest man I'd ever met decided to lean close and talk to me." She looked down at Haydn, whose eyes looked suspiciously shiny. "And my life hasn't been the same since."

She ran her fingers over her guitar, and a piano behind her started playing an introduction.

"Tonight, I want to play for you a song that's never been heard before now, in honor of that person I met, and how my life has changed. It's easy to think that when things are bad, they're never going to get good again, but that's not true. There are always good things waiting for us around the corner, even in our most turbulent times."

She paused, feeling her own eyes sting with tears. This was ridiculous. This song wasn't a crying song. But it was incredible to think how far she'd come in the last year since she'd gone to Alaska. She had an amazing relationship with her dad, Marissa, and her siblings. She had gained three best friends with Rosie, Jules, and Bennett.

And Haydn, her perpetual sunshine.

"So, here's my new song, 'Turbulent.'"

She started to sing the terrible, repeating lyrics, where every line ending rhymed with "turbulent." By the second time through the chorus, the crowd had caught on and they were singing along with her, their hands in the air over their heads.

She laughed as she finished the final note and everyone screamed. "Thank you. Now, who wants to hear the real songs from the island album?" She jumped right into singing her song about the abandoned cabin, her eyes drawn to Haydn's again and again.

Everyone had left her house except for Haydn. Lia was a mix between exhausted and ramped up after her concert. She'd see everyone again tomorrow, but for now, she wasn't sad to see them all go to their hotels. She was craving some alone time with Haydn.

They were sitting in a couple of outside lounge chairs they'd dragged from the patio to the grass, and they were holding hands as they stared up at the stars. It was nothing like the brilliant and expansive Alaska night sky, but it was hers, and she was with the person she loved, so it felt absolutely perfect.

Haydn pulled her hand up to his mouth and kissed her knuckles. "I could watch you every day for the rest of my life."

"I could watch you every day for the rest of my life too." Lia turned to face him, and she found Haydn sitting up in the chair, the ring box in his shaking hand. Her heart skipped a beat, and she sat up as well, her knees pressed to his.

"I was going to wait for the perfect time—"

"This is the perfect time," Lia interrupted to say.

He looked surprised, and then he smiled, biting his bottom lip as he did so. "Lia, I love you. I can't imagine one more day of this ... turbulent life without you."

"Me neither."

He leaned close enough that their lips were almost touching. "Will you marry me?"

"I thought you'd never ask," she breathed against his mouth.

He grinned and kissed her, before slipping a ring onto her finger. It was a gorgeous pearl surrounded by diamonds. She loved it. She loved him.

And now she had another verse to add to her turbulent

song. *My last year was turbulent, but it ended in an amazing engagement.*

It needed some work, but so did all the best things in life.

Read Rosie's love story next!
It is a truth universally acknowledged that a hockey player in possession of a bad reputation must be in want of a fake girlfriend.

Rosie Forrester is in desperate need of cash after an embarrassing run-in with the law. Enter Dylan Savage, a disgraced hockey player who needs a place to hide out for a few months while he figures out how to get back on his team.

He's every bit as beastly as his fans' nickname for him would imply—nothing like the handsome, *charming* bookstore owner Rosie's in love with from afar. But Dylan's rent will not only save her art studio, it'll help fund the secret she's keeping from her three older brothers.

When Rosie proposes a deal to help Dylan improve his image if he can help her finally catch the eye of the bookstore owner, he reluctantly agrees. But nothing in their plan is going as expected, and pretty soon it's not just her studio she's worried about losing, it's her heart.

Rosie and The Beast Next Door is for readers who love Jane Austen, forced proximity, banter, hockey players, fake dating, and happily ever afters!

KAYLEE BALDWIN

Rosie and The Beast Next Door

ROSIE AND THE BEAST NEXT DOOR
CHAPTER 1

Forrester Sibling Group Chat

HAYDN

What was the name of that movie Rosie made
us watch last year at the cabin?

HAYDN

The one with the long dresses and all that
weird dancing.

JULES

Was it *about* dresses?

HAYDN

No. It was a love story though. They did lots of
walking.

HAYDN

Rosie went on and on about how sexy hand
flexing was when the movie was over.

JULES

I remember that! *shudders*

ROSIE

PRIDE AND PREJUDICE!!

How have I failed my brothers so terribly?

BENNETT

I remembered. I was just getting ready to type it, but you were too quick.

JULES

Riiiiight.

ROSIE

Why do you need to know, Haydn?

HAYDN

Lia and I were talking about movies with ridiculous plotlines, and I couldn't remember the name.

JULES

It was SO ridiculous. What guy proposes a SECOND time after being told no? Where's your self-respect, Mr. Doofus?

ROSIE

MR. DARCY.

HAYDN

And all the long, drawn out pasture scenes? Snooze.

ROSIE

I have disowned you all. Dissing Pride and Prejudice is too much.

JULES

You know whose hand flex I liked? Thanos.

HAYDN

Dude, that movie was so good. That hand flex actually meant something.

ROSIE

You mean the one that killed half the world?

JULES

Exactly.

BENNETT

It was more of a snap than a flex.

JULES

Taking out half the world was totally a flex.

ROSIE

Do NOT ruin the handflex for me.

JULES

handflex

ROSIE

UGH!

Please check your email at your earliest convenience as you will find a "special" invitation for all of you.

I await your RSVP.

Revenge was a dish best served while watching the six-hour version of *Pride and Prejudice* with my three older brothers.

"I was promised a hand-flex," Jules said through the lap top screen.

Since we lived in three different states—Alaska, Tennessee, and Washington—we'd continued our long-held family tradition of movie night on the first Friday of the month via video chat. Most of the time I wished we could all be together, but with Jules unable to sit still for the length of a regular movie, much less a six hour one, it was kind of nice to turn the laptop away from my line of vision so his movements didn't distract me.

"That's the other one. The shorter version," Bennett said distractedly. He was on the floor of my apartment, working on a puzzle he'd set up on the coffee table. No, my brother wasn't a retiree, just a twenty-eight-year-old, bearded fisherman who also happened to love a good puzzle in his free time.

"Shhhhh," I said. "This is the good part."

"You've said that every time we talk," Jules mumbled.

I was sprawled on my futon, one hand dangling down to rest in the popcorn bowl for easy access. "It's *all* good parts."

"We missed the Peaks hockey game," Haydn said. He had his phone way too close to his face and at an unflattering angle, as usual, and in the dark room, the light from the movie kept changing his skin tone to shades of blue. He'd become a huge fan of the Peaks when two players from our small Alaskan town had been signed. *Everyone* in town was a fan of the Peaks. It was a requirement, even if we had mixed feelings for their star player, Dylan Savage.

"You have no one to blame but yourself for this mess," I reminded him as I watched Elizabeth and Mr. Darcy walk awkwardly around Pemberley. As much as I would have appreciated watching Dylan Savage skate around the rink like he owned the place (and I *definitely* appreciated it), I would settle for nothing less than a Mr. Darcy.

Plus I never gave up an opportunity to mess with my brothers.

The boys quieted as Lydia and Wickham's relationship and supposed elopement came to light, and when Darcy and Elizabeth got together in the end, I wasn't the only one who sighed.

There was a chance the boys were sighing in relief, but really, what would they do without me?

Thanks to me, they'd watched every classic nineties rom-com and could quote Norah Ephron while catching fish or playing basketball or doing any other manly thing they insisted they loved doing whenever women came around. Every time a girl swooned for one of them, I patted myself on the back.

Once we'd finished the rom-coms, we'd moved on to musicals and period pieces. I was debating entering our Aubrey Hepburn era next.

Did they ever get to choose the movies for family movie night?

Nope.

Did I feel bad about that?

Also nope.

My oldest brother, Haydn, had raised me since Dad left and Mom died—when he'd barely been an adult himself—sacrificing his own dreams for so long, he forgot how to have them. Bennett and Jules stepped up as well, and as a result I was smothered with protective father figures who still saw me as the trembling nine-year-old clutching a stuffed otter at our mom's funeral, even if I was now a full-grown twenty-four year old. I loved them. I loved getting under their skin. Teasing was our collective love language.

Besides, there were privileges to being the baby. Privileges I took full advantage of. Like secretly listing their vacation cabin as a short term rental to earn some extra money—which was a fantastic idea, by the way, until I rented it out to famous country singer, Lia Halifax, on the same weekend my brothers unexpectedly showed up for a weekend getaway. But since Lia and Haydn were married now, I felt like instead of them bringing it up as a reminder of how my good intentions often led to loads of problems, they should be thanking me. Praising me. Asking me to use my mad genius to get the rest of them married off to women as fantastic as Lia.

And then the man of my dreams—Winterhaven's dreamy bookstore owner—would fall in love with me, too, and we'd all live happily ever after.

Continue reading Rosie's story...

ABOUT THE AUTHOR

Kaylee Baldwin's love of all things books and reading led her to graduate from Arizona State University with a degree in English. She writes romantic comedies with tons of heart (and literary references, because she is fundamentally a book nerd.) She lives in Arizona with her family, and adores traveling, finding gluten-free recipes that are actually delicious, and pretending she's actually going to read all the books she buys.

ALSO BY KAYLEE BALDWIN

Enchanted Forresters

Me and Mr. Just Right

Rosie and the Beast Next Door

Amelia and Her Prince Charming

Evie and The Big Bad Bodyguard

Christmas

Snowed In at Jingle Falls

Take My Heart

Diamond Cove

A Summer Mismatch

A Wedding Mismatch

Billionaire Cove

Her Billionaire Rival

Her Billionaire Heartthrob